MAKING BOOKS

An Imprint of Abdo Publishing
abdobooks.com

BY ALEXIS BURLING

abdobooks.com

Printed in the United States of America, North Mankato, Minnesota.
052024
092024

Cover Photos: Shutterstock Images (books); Ahmet Misirligul/Shutterstock Images (pencil); Zaytseva Larisa/Shutterstock Images (writing); Praphan Jampala/Shutterstock Images (keyboard)
Interior Photos: Zaytseva Larisa/Shutterstock Images, 1 (left); Praphan Jampala/Shutterstock Images, 1 (right); Fajrul Islam/Moment/Getty Images, 4; Shutterstock Images, 8, 11, 41, 54, 70, 86, 100; Stuart Ramson/Alliance for Young Artists & Writers/AP Images, 13; Amir Makar/AFP/Getty Images, 14; Heritage Art/Heritage Images/Hulton Archive/Getty Images, 17; Werner Otto/Alamy, 18; Hulton Archive/Getty Images, 21; PA Images/Alamy, 22; Emmanuel Dunand/AFP/Getty Images, 27; Maskot/DigitalVision/Getty Images, 28; Erin Clark/Boston Globe/Getty Images, 31; Albert Llop/NurPhoto SRL/Alamy Live News/Alamy, 32; Eamonn McCabe/Popperfoto/Getty Images, 35; Daniel Boczarski/Getty Images Entertainment/Getty Images, 36–37; Roberto Machado Noa/LightRocket/Getty Images, 42; BooksR/Alamy, 45; Sebastian Gollnow/picture-alliance/dpa/AP Images, 48–49; Sebastian Christoph Gollnow/dpa picture alliance/Alamy, 50; Desiree Navarro/FilmMagic/Getty Images, 53; Justin Sullivan/Getty Images News/Getty Images, 57; Jeffrey Whyte/Alamy, 60; Lubo Ivanko/Shutterstock Images, 61; Johnny Louis/Getty Images Entertainment/Getty Images, 63; Carlos Avila Gonzalez/The San Francisco Chronicle/Hearst Newspapers/Getty Images, 64; Postmodern Studio/Alamy, 66; Bill Watters/Getty Images Entertainment/Getty Images, 69; Sam Mellish/In Pictures/Getty Images, 73; Asier Romero/Shutterstock Images, 78; David Kohl/AP Images, 81; Randy Shropshire/Getty Images for PEN America/Getty Images Entertainment/Getty Images, 82; Unique Nicole/Getty Images Entertainment/Getty Images, 89; Thaspol Sangsee/Shutterstock Images, 90; Jeff Kravitz/FilmMagic for HBO/FilmMagic/Getty Images, 95; Rick Bowmer/AP Images, 96; Dimitrios Kambouris/Getty Images for WSJ. Magazine Innovators Awards/Getty Images Entertainment/Getty Images, 99; Tada Images/Shutterstock Images, 101

Editor: Laura Stickney
Series Designer: Maggie Villaume

Library of Congress Control Number: 2023949555

Publisher's Cataloging-in-Publication Data
Names: Burling, Alexis, author.
Title: Making books / by Alexis Burling
Description: Minneapolis, Minnesota: Abdo Publishing, 2025 | Series: Making media | Includes online resources and index.
Identifiers: ISBN 9781098293345 (lib. bdg.) | ISBN 9798384912613 (ebook)
Subjects: LCSH: Publishers and publishing--Juvenile literature. | Writing (Authorship)--Juvenile literature. | Books--Juvenile literature. | Bookbinding--Juvenile literature.
Classification: DDC 028--dc23

CONTENTS

CHAPTER **ONE**

A CREATIVE JOURNEY

Ever since Devon was a kid, he loved stringing words together to create something meaningful. At every family gathering, his mom told anyone who would listen that as soon as Devon could talk, he spoke in rhymes. "The fat cat sat on the hat," she would say. "Can you believe it? We didn't even have a cat!"

As Devon grew older, his obsession with rhymes rose to a whole new level. His mom bought him a blank notebook so he could write down poems whenever he got inspired. While shooting hoops in the park, Devon and his friend Jamal would see who could come up with the best rhymes on the fly. Before long, they had an audience of friends and neighbors who loved hearing them create poetry on demand.

Devon's mom and friends weren't his only fans. Devon's teachers noticed his skills too. His English teacher, Mrs. Shugart, always told Devon he was talented. In fact, throughout Devon's entire junior year of high school, Mrs. Shugart had

Many writers recommend carrying a writing notebook, or commonplace book. Writers use this type of notebook to jot down ideas, sketches, quotes, and poems.

THE SCHOLASTIC ART & WRITING AWARDS

Founded in 1923, the Scholastic Art & Writing Awards is the longest-running arts award program for teens in the United States. Teens in grades 7 through 12 can apply. The contest consists of 28 categories of art and writing, including poetry, novels, flash fiction, journalism, digital art, sculpture, photography, and printmaking. Entry fees are $10 per individual entry and $30 per portfolio.[1] Winners can receive scholarships to summer programs, college tuition assistance, or cash prizes. There is a national awards ceremony every year, as well as regional, national, and traveling exhibitions. Some winners' work is also published in art catalogs and writing anthology publications.

encouraged him to submit poems to the school's literary magazine. She also told him about a national contest for teens sponsored by the publishing company Scholastic. It was called the Scholastic Art & Writing Awards.

"You might want to submit a poem or even a portfolio in September," Mrs. Shugart said. "The worst that could happen is that you don't win anything. But something might come of it. It's worth a shot."

CREATING A PORTFOLIO

Devon thought about what Mrs. Shugart had said. He hadn't considered his knack for creating poetry to be a talent. It was just something he liked to do in his spare time. Writing poems made Devon feel less anxious when he was worried about things, such as applying to colleges or the threat of climate change. Writing about his mom's nasty meatloaf or his sister's latest boyfriend was also a way to make his family laugh. Unlike other school subjects that Devon struggled to get right, poetry just came naturally to him.

Devon wasn't sure if he should enter the contest. But his girlfriend, Shayna, finally persuaded him to make a portfolio and give the Scholastic Art & Writing Awards a try. Devon decided to go one step further. He planned to create an actual book featuring six of his best poems.

He would submit the book in addition to another six poems that he'd send in as independent entries. Devon had no idea how to start the book creation process. But instead of overthinking it, he decided to dive right into the work.

First, Devon flipped through the notebook his mom had given him seven months ago. He picked out the poems he liked best. Some were very personal—one was about falling in love, while another was about losing his grandmother.

Others tackled topics that Devon was learning about in school, such as gun control and the Black Lives Matter movement. After he'd picked out a few older poems, Devon wrote a few new ones about visiting his dad's side of the family in Puerto Rico. At the last minute, he added another poem about his mother's meatloaf—because no matter how hard he tried to like it, it really was nasty.

> **"We can say for certain then that a program like [The Scholastic Art & Writing Awards] doesn't just honor artists. It creates them. It nurtures them. It gives them permission to shine brighter, to think differently, to be bolder.[2]"**
>
> ***—Jennifer Garner, actress and host of the 2020 Scholastic Art & Writing Awards ceremony***

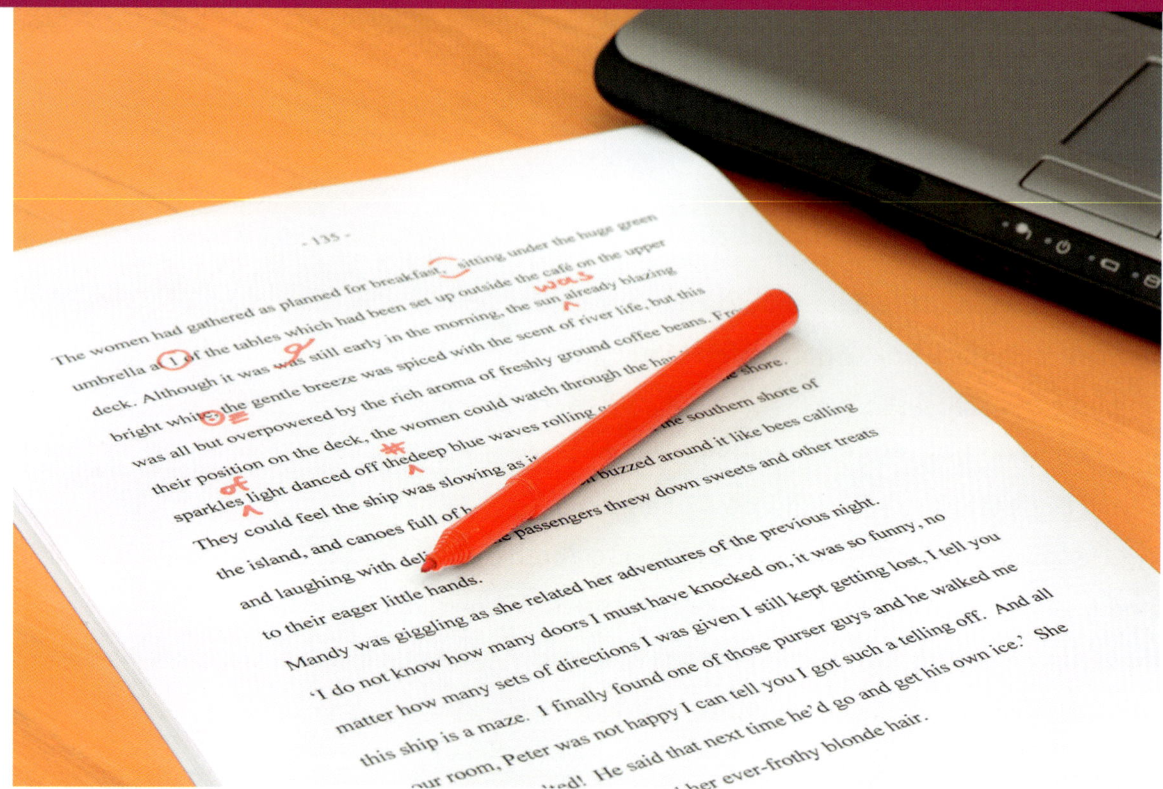

Some writers edit by marking up a paper copy of their work. They may check for spelling and punctuation errors. They may also add or delete sentences from the text.

Devon spent weeks rereading and editing his poems. He searched for typos, incorrect punctuation, and words that seemed overly fancy or out of place. He read each poem out loud to fine-tune the pacing of the lines. He even scrapped a poem that seemed too cheesy and rewrote it from scratch.

After about a month, Devon finally felt like the poems were ready. He gathered up his poems and showed them to the people he trusted most: his mom, his sister, Jamal, and Mrs. Shugart. He asked each of them for feedback. Then he went to the library to check out a bunch of recent poetry books published by renowned publishers, such as Graywolf Press.

He paged through the books to get a sense of how they were formatted. He noticed that the books had lots of white space around the edges of the text to prevent crowding and give the poems room to breathe. Finally, Devon did a little research online. He read a few articles about how to make a book that was simple and inexpensive but still looked professional.

WHAT IS A PORTFOLIO?

A portfolio is a physical or digital collection of an artist's or writer's original work. It usually includes pieces of writing that represent a writer's range of skills. A portfolio also showcases who a writer is as an artist and demonstrates their interests. Most artist portfolios consist of ten to 20 pieces, examples, or published clips.[3] Having a portfolio allows artists to keep their work all in one place. It also makes it easier to apply for jobs, contests, scholarships, schools, and other opportunities.

MAKING A BOOK

Devon knew his goal wasn't to publish a book on his own—at least not yet. For now, he just wanted to create a beautiful product that might impress the judges at the Scholastic Art & Writing Awards. Depending on what happened with the contest, Devon might submit some of his work to literary magazines such as the *Adroit Journal*. Or he might contact publishers about his poetry at a later date, when he knew more about the publishing process. That way, he would have a larger body of work to choose from.

> **I'm writing a first draft and reminding myself that I'm simply shoveling sand into a box so that later I can build castles.[4]**
>
> ***—Shannon Hale, author, on revising and editing***

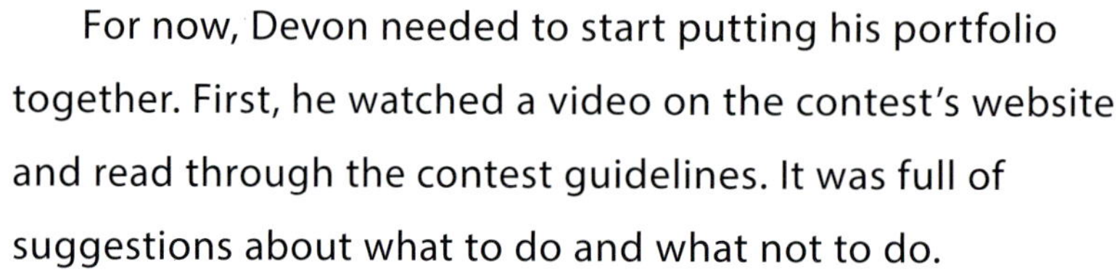

For now, Devon needed to start putting his portfolio together. First, he watched a video on the contest's website and read through the contest guidelines. It was full of suggestions about what to do and what not to do.

Then he typed up all his poems in Microsoft Word using the required 12-point Times New Roman font. He then made sure the margins on each numbered page were correct. Next, he created a table of contents and a title page. He ran a spell-check to make sure there weren't any typos. Finally, Devon uploaded everything into Calibre, a free e-book creation software program.

For the final step, Devon asked Jamal to send him the portrait Jamal had created for art class. It was a profile of Devon sitting on a basketball court, staring into the sunset. The image captured the moodiness of the poems in Devon's book and conveyed a lot about his personality without saying a word. It was the perfect image for the book's cover.

THE FINAL VERDICT

Devon spent four months preparing his poetry book. As soon as the contest submission period opened in September, Devon created an account on the Scholastic Art & Writing

Awards portal. He uploaded six poems as individual entries. Then he submitted his poetry book as part of his senior writing portfolio.

He also included the other two documents the contest required. One was a writer statement, which described Devon's process for curating his poetry portfolio. The other was a personal statement, which explained who Devon was as a person. After he pressed Submit, all he could do was sit back and wait.

Devon waited for six months to find out the results of the contest. He spent time on his college applications and tried to do well in school. He and Jamal played basketball every weekend while shouting poems to each other across the court.

By March, Devon had nearly forgotten about the contest. But then he found out the unbelievable news. Out of more than 340,000 total submissions to the contest, Devon was one of 16 high school seniors who received a Gold Medal Portfolio Award. The prize came with a $10,000 scholarship.[5] In June, Devon would also get to attend an awards ceremony at Carnegie Hall in New York City.

As soon as he found out the news, the first thing he did was tell his mom. "Mom! You won't believe it!" Devon screamed downstairs from his bedroom. "I won!" The next thing Devon did was text Jamal, who demanded they

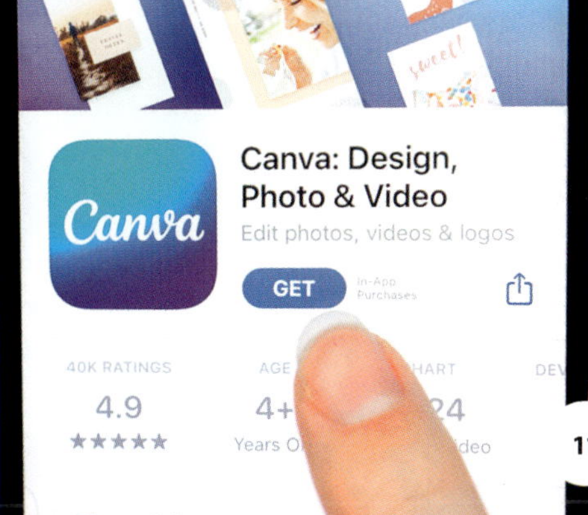

Writers can use many different e-book creation tools, such as Canva. This platform allows users to easily design their own graphics, book covers, and e-books.

celebrate immediately. The following day, Devon ran into Mrs. Shugart's office before school started and gave her a massive hug.

"Sorry for the surprise hug, Mrs. S., but I really couldn't have done it without you," Devon told Mrs. Shugart. "Thanks for believing in me and making this all happen."

"Oh, I didn't make anything happen," Mrs. Shugart replied. "That was all you, Devon. It was you—and your talent—who won the prize. You did it all on your own."

THE NATIONAL STUDENT POETS PROGRAM

There are many different writing programs and contests for students of all ages. Poets in grades 10 and 11 can be nominated to participate in the National Student Poets Program. The winners of the program serve as youth poetry ambassadors. They take part in a variety of individual service projects, April Poetry Month readings, and workshops around the country. The ambassadors may also attend national poetry conferences and festivals.

A FUTURE OF POSSIBILITIES

Devon was over the moon about winning a Scholastic Art & Writing Award. It made him feel confident about his writing. It also inspired him to think about writing more poetry or even trying other writing styles.

After Devon traveled to New York City and met some of the contest judges, he also began to think more seriously about creating longer poetry books in the future. Maybe he'd use a different software program. He could try to sell some of his self-published work through online retailers, such as Amazon. Or he could submit his portfolio to literary magazines or publishers

During the Scholastic Art & Writing Awards National Ceremony, students who receive Gold Medal Portfolio Awards are invited onstage. The event also features speeches by famous writers and celebrities.

to get feedback from professionals—and maybe even a shot at a publishing contract. Devon didn't know what the future would bring. First he had to think about college. But still, after winning such a prestigious writing award, Devon felt hopeful and tremendously inspired. For now, that was all that mattered.

THE HISTORY OF BOOKS

Today, there are plenty of options for book lovers looking for something to read. They can buy printed novels or biographies from bookstores. They can study textbooks in classrooms. They can even read digital graphic novels on a laptop or smartphone. There is a seemingly endless supply of reading material available. One study found that in 2021, three million new books were published in the United States. About 2.3 million of those were self-published.[1]

But books weren't always so readily available. Early books weren't even printed on paper. The craft of creating books has been around for thousands of years, and it has changed significantly during that time.

ANCIENT SCROLLS

Most historians trace the origins of books to Mesopotamia and ancient Egypt, likely between 3500 and 3000 BCE. These texts were written on different surfaces, including leather, stone, metal, and bone. Ancient Sumerians in Mesopotamia wrote

People can see ancient papyrus scrolls on display at the Egyptian Museum in Cairo, Egypt.

CODICES

Codices were some of the earliest book manuscripts. *Codex* is Latin for "block of wood." Between 100 and 300 CE, Romans began sewing folded sheets of papyrus or parchment together. They bound the sheets between wooden covers. These codices were useful because they could be opened to any page, unlike scrolls that had to be unrolled. They could also have text on both sides of the pages. Codices eventually replaced papyrus scrolls as a popular way of reading.

symbols on tablets made of clay. They created writing instruments out of reeds and used them to make deep impressions in the clay. Then they dried the clay in the sun or in a kiln, which preserved the markings.

Beginning around 2400 BCE, people in Egypt made books from papyrus. This grasslike aquatic plant grew in the Nile Valley. People wove pieces of papyrus together like a mat. Then they glued or sewed the woven pieces together to create long scrolls to write on. At that time, an average Egyptian scroll was around 30 feet (9 m) long and seven to ten inches (18–25 cm) wide. The longest Egyptian scroll ever found stretches more than 133 feet (40.5 m). That's nearly as tall as the Statue of Liberty.[2]

By around 600 BCE, other book formats had grown in popularity. In Ancient Greece, people created parchment out of treated animal skin. This material was more durable than papyrus, and people could write on both sides of it.

NEW PRINTING INNOVATIONS

By 700 CE, new innovations in printing had developed. During the Tang Dynasty in China, people carved symbols into sheets of wood. Then they covered the wood with ink

During the medieval period, European monks often created illuminated manuscripts. These featured intricate illustrations, decorative borders, and golden detailing.

made from plant and animal dyes mixed with water or wine. A sheet of paper was then pressed onto the wood to create a woodblock print. People used this method to print Buddhist prayers and spiritual teachings. The earliest example of a dated, printed book is a Buddhist text called the *Diamond Sutra* from 868 CE.

Around this time, scribes in Europe wrote texts by hand, especially in monasteries. The largest monasteries had rooms called scriptoria, where monks copied and illustrated volumes. Medieval manuscripts were so valuable that some scribes placed hexes on the books. These hexes were meant to punish anyone who stole or damaged a manuscript.

DAS
NEUE
TESTA
MENT

One example is in a copy of the Vulgate, a Latin translation of the Bible. It had a hex printed on one of its pages. The hex read, "Whoever steals this book let him die the death; let be him be frizzled in a pan; may the falling sickness rage within him; may he be broken on the wheel and be hanged."[3]

A GROUNDBREAKING INVENTION

Because books had to be written by hand, they were time-consuming to create. This made books expensive. Usually, only wealthy people and church officials had access to books. Most people could not read. In 1440, only around 30 percent of adults in Europe knew how to read.[4]

In 1448, German goldsmith Johannes Gutenberg created a machine with metal squares that could be moved around to create words. The concept of movable type had been around for a few hundred years. A wooden system was developed in China in the 1040s, and a metal version surfaced in Korea in the 1230s. But Gutenberg was the first to expand the invention to a larger audience.

Instead of water-based dye, which didn't stick to metal, he used oil-based ink made with lamp soot, turpentine, and walnut oil. In 1455, he printed his first book, the Gutenberg Bible. It brought about what became known as Europe's Gutenberg Revolution, paving the way for the commercial printing of books on a mass scale.

The Gutenberg printing press featured two wooden plates that pressed paper and movable type together. The University of Münster in Germany has a replica of the press.

THE FIRST DUST JACKET

Before the 1800s, books were often wrapped in leather or silk to protect their ornate, fragile covers. But in 1829, the first detachable paper book cover was conceived. It was for a gift book called *Friendship's Offering* and was sealed with wax. Gift books were highly decorated volumes that contained poems, pictures, and stories. "These books were . . . often bound very nicely and probably in silk," says Clive Hurst, a rare book librarian. "Silk bindings are very vulnerable to wear and tear and handling so booksellers would keep them in these wrappers to protect the silk binding underneath."[8]

Gutenberg's printing press made creating books easier and more efficient. Multiple identical editions of a book could be printed in a short period of time. By the end of the 1500s, printing shops had sprouted throughout Europe. There were about 300 printing shops in Germany alone.[5]

Before the printing press was invented, the total number of books in Europe was around 30,000. By 1500, that number had grown to 12 million.[6] This led to increased literacy rates in Europe. In 1641, about 30 percent of people in England were literate. By 1696, that number had grown to 47 percent.[7]

A LITERARY MAKEOVER

Books in the 1600s, 1700s, and 1800s looked similar, but not identical, to modern books. Until the late 1400s, book covers were made of wood or paper sheets pasted together into a block. A type of board made of rope fibers became a less expensive option for book covers.

Modern hardcover books have a slightly rounded spine to hold pages together. But 300 years ago, most book spines were flat. Flat book spines split more easily, but people preferred them because they allowed a book to rest flat on a table for easy reading.

In 1744, Swedish chemist Carl Wilhelm Scheele discovered that a combination of hydrochloric acid and manganese dioxide produced a gas that could be used to make bleach. In 1810, inventor Sir Humphry Davy named the gas chlorine. The chemists' discoveries led to the practice of bleaching paper, which gives book pages a clean, white appearance.

THE PAPERBACK IS BORN

In the mid-1800s, the world of books continued to evolve. The first mass-market paperback books were created in Britain. These pamphlet-like books were printed on cheap pulp paper and usually cost a penny.

No. 1.] Nos. 2, 3 and 4 are Presented, Gratis, with this No. [Price 1d.

VARNEY THE VAMPIRE OR THE FEAST OF BLOOD

A ROMANCE OF EXCITING INTEREST.

BY THE AUTHOR OF "GRACE RIVERS; OR, THE MERCHANT'S DAUGHTER."

In Britain, inexpensive mass-market books were often called penny dreadfuls. Many penny dreadfuls, such as *Varney the Vampire*, featured violent tales of crime and adventure.

PAINTING AND SCULPTURE IN EUROPE 1780-1880
The Pelican History of Art
HEALTH AND HORMONES
A Pelican Book
INTRUDER IN THE DUST
LADY CHATTERLEY'S LOVER
D.H. LAWRENCE
THE LAST TYCOON
F. Scott Fitzgerald
Dishonoured Bones
NANCY MITFORD
Voltaire in Love
Penguin Biography
Cooking
Philip Harben

They included Gothic thrillers such as *Sweeney Todd* and *Varney the Vampire*. These types of books were sometimes serialized in weekly parts. They quickly caught on with working class people. Soon, the phenomenon spread to the United States. Wild West stories such as *Buffalo Bill* were a big hit there. Americans called these books dime novels. Many were based on stories from daily newspapers and featured recurring characters. By the 1880s, the Wild West genre had given way to detective novels.

Full-length novels at the time were usually published and sold in three separate volumes. This way, publishing houses could make a better profit. But three-volume novels were often too expensive for the average reader. Most people obtained books through lending libraries, such as the Mudie's Select Library. Customers paid a one-year fee to borrow books

Some authors also chose to serialize their novels in literary magazines, publishing them in monthly installments. British author Charles Dickens published many novels in this way. Serializing novels made them more accessible to the general reading public and provided a more affordable option.

Over time, big book-publishing companies began to form across Europe and the United States. One of the earliest publishers was created in 1817. Long Island shop owner Joseph Harper gave his sons money to start a printing business. Over time, it grew into HarperCollins, one of the most successful publishing companies. Publishing company

In the 1930s, Sir Allen Lane helped popularize paperback books. He founded Penguin Books, which offered affordable, high-quality paperbacks.

Doubleday was founded in 1897. The next year, it published its first bestseller, Rudyard Kipling's *The Day's Work*. By the mid-1900s, book sales were going strong, especially in New York.

For the next 50 years, paperbacks were considered to be lower quality than hardcover books. But in 1935, a risky business maneuver changed how people thought about paperbacks. Sir Allen Lane purchased the rights to 10 respected titles. He printed 20,000 copies at a time to keep costs down. A retail chain named Woolworths bought 63,000 copies of the books. It sold out of all of them.[9]

On the heels of this success, Lane created Penguin Books in 1936. Ten months later, Penguin Books had printed one million paperbacks.[10] Within a few years, Penguin expanded into other imprints, including Puffin for children's books and Pelican for educational nonfiction books.

BOOKS GO DIGITAL

Beginning in the 1980s, new inventions transformed the way books were sold and read. As technology advanced, companies began offering books in digital formats. In 1985, the *New Grolier Electronic Encyclopedia* was the first book published on a compact disc (CD). Jeff Bezos launched the first online bookstore out of his garage in 1995. It became Amazon, a multibillion-dollar business.

Two years later, Audible.com introduced the first portable digital audio player for audiobooks. Soon sellers were offering books as e-books. In 1997, Martin Eberhard and Marc Tarpenning created the Rocketbook, the first e-reader device. Users could download books onto it.

In 2000, Stephen King's novella *Riding the Bullet* became one of the first books to be published as an e-book. That same year, King became the first major author to self-publish a book on the internet in installments. In 2007, the Amazon Kindle became the world's first widely popular e-book reader device. It sold out in less than six hours.[11]

Print-on-demand companies also began to form. These companies print copies of a book only when they receive orders for the book. This allows authors to print a precise number of books they need. Lightning Source, one of the largest print-on-demand companies, was founded in 1997, followed by self-publishing outfits iUniverse, CreateSpace, and Lulu.

THE FIRST AUDIOBOOKS

In 1932, the audiobook was created to help blind people read books. The American Foundation of the Blind recorded books read aloud on vinyl records. After World War II (1939–1945), when many soldiers returned home with damaged eyesight, these "talking-books" grew in popularity. Each record had 15 minutes of audio recorded on each side.[12] Some of the first talking-books included plays by William Shakespeare, the US Constitution, and Gladys Hasty Carroll's novel *As the Earth Turns*.

After that, people inside and outside the publishing industry speculated about how the publishing business might change. They wondered how new technology would

> **[Twenty] or 30 years from now, there's going to be some gizmo that kids carry around in their back pocket that has everything in it—including our books, if they want.[14]**
>
> ***—Michael Stern Hart, founder of the Project Gutenberg digital library, 1998***

affect printed books. They also wondered how the power to self-publish might transform the publishing world—for better or for worse.

Through 2023, hardcover and paperback book sales were still going strong. In 2022, more than 788 million books were sold in the United States. More than 224 million were hardcovers, and more than 448 million were paperbacks. About 31 million were mass-market paperbacks, while 48 million were children's board books.[13]

Today, the publishing business continues to change. Vellum, Kindle Create, and other software programs help writers release and sell books to the public without having to work with traditional publishers. Social media platforms such as Goodreads help both self-published authors and traditionally published authors spread word about their books.

Some writers even use artificial intelligence (AI) to help them write summaries for book jackets. No one knows for sure which methods will stick or how the publishing business will change in the decades ahead. But the art of making and reading books certainly isn't going away any time soon.

Amazon has released several different versions of the Kindle, including the Kindle Paperwhite and the Kindle Oasis. Users can download e-books directly to these devices.

kindle
12:07
Newsstand
Books
Music
Video
Docs
Apps
Web
marie claire
amazon
Angry Birds ...
amazon

CREATING A MANUSCRIPT

There are plenty of reasons to write a book, and there are many kinds of books to create. Some people write memoirs to share life stories or experiences. Others write about important world events, such as a natural disaster or historical milestones. They might choose to write a nonfiction book about a celebrity, such as Argentine soccer player Lionel Messi.

Some writers enjoy imagining casts of characters living complex or fantastical lives. They write fiction, fantasy, or science fiction books. They might write short stories or novels for kids or teens. Other writers are also talented visual artists. They might create graphic novels with intricately drawn panels. Or they might write and illustrate picture books for young readers.

Whichever literary style a writer chooses, creating a book is hard work. Although the path to publication is long and sometimes full of rejection, most writers say the journey is worth it. Bestselling author George Saunders spoke about navigating the difficult parts of the writing process. "The antidote, for me, has been getting

To come up with writing ideas, people can use online writing prompts or plot generators. They can also read other writers' work and do writing exercises in a journal.

LITERARY GENRES

There are four main genres, or types, of literature. These are fiction, nonfiction, plays, and poetry. There are many subgenres within each category. For example, fiction writers can explore fantasy, science fiction, historical fiction, horror, thrillers, or romance. Nonfiction writers may write autobiographies, memoirs, essay collections, or travelogues. Playwrights can script tragedies, comedies, or tragicomedies. A poet might write haiku, limericks, sonnets, or free-verse poems.

comfortable with my own revision process—seeing those bad first lines as just a starting place," he said. "If you know the path you'll take from bad to better to good, you don't get so dismayed by the initial mess."[1]

FINDING AN IDEA

Writing a book can be daunting. It requires energy and discipline. Even established writers say that sitting down to write can be challenging, and the process isn't always fun. Alice Munro is a bestselling Canadian author. "Writing is hard," she said. "But the more you write, and enjoy what you write, the better it gets."[2]

The first step in making a book is finding an idea. If thinking up ideas doesn't come easily, writers can use tools to assist with the process. Websites such as RanGen and Seventh Sanctum offer online plot generators. These tools help people come up with story ideas. Other companies, such as *Writer's Digest* and the *New York Times*, publish creative writing prompts daily to get writers' creative juices flowing.

Many publishing experts recommend that writers ask themselves questions while going through the brainstorming process. For example, a writer might ask, "If I could

Writers can brainstorm ideas by creating outlines, lists, or story maps. They may practice these skills in writing classes or workshops.

Scene heading
Slugline
1 min a page
Courier
Action
What characters are doing
Camera
Final Draft
FADE IN:
EXT. CITY - DAY
Action lines
Grey faceless building.
A lifeless city center.
if they are empty.
INT. (interior)
exterior)
DAY
NIGHT
DUSK
DAWN

For some writers, the research process involves collecting historical documents, artifacts, and photos. Some writers may also read books, interview experts, or travel to places they want to write about.

write about anything in the world, what would it be?" A writer might also consider whether they will be able to carry out their idea effectively and who their potential audience is.

Whatever the idea may be, it's best to pick one that will sustain itself throughout the writing process. "There are many horrible reasons for choosing what you're going to write about, and only one correct reason," says Nathan Bransford, author of *How to Write a Novel*. "The horrible reasons are almost always variations of one basic and colossal mistake, which is that you are choosing a particular idea because you think it will make you mountains of money. . . . The only reason for choosing something to write about is because you love . . . the idea."[3]

> **When you do find the right idea, you'll know it. You'll just know. It will beat you over the head with its rightness and make you feel like you're skipping through a tulip field while hugging a puppy, because you will have finally found an idea you love enough to turn into a novel.**[4]
>
> ***—Nathan Bransford, author***

DOING THE RESEARCH

Once a writer has chosen an idea, the writing process can begin. But most writers can't just sit down and write a perfect novel or short story—not even a famous and successful writer. Even if a writer knows what style of book they want to write, they must first familiarize themselves with examples of that style to get a sense of how it is written. This means reading as much as possible. Librarians are a great source for book recommendations. Bestseller lists are helpful starting points too.

During the research process, writers should think about big-picture aspects, such as narrative structure, chapter placement, character development, and point of view. They should study how other authors use these tools. "Read, read, read. Read everything—trash, classics, good and bad, and see how they do it," said author William Faulkner. "Just like a carpenter who works as an apprentice and studies the master. Read! You'll absorb it. Then write. If it's good, you'll find out. If it's not, throw it out of the window."[5]

Most editors and publishing representatives suggest that new authors also think about whether their book will bring anything new to the table. For example, an author might write a story that is a new twist on an old idea. Publishers and readers want to see books that offer fresh perspectives and new ideas.

WRITING THE MANUSCRIPT

There are many ways to create a manuscript. Some authors use storyboards to map out each scene and keep track of how their story is progressing from one scene to the next. Others stick Post-it notes on the wall and move them around to figure out their book's plot or timeline. Whichever method a writer uses, creating an outline is one way to keep

Many authors have special writing spaces or writing rooms. Having a designated writing space can help a writer create a routine and concentrate on their work.

a book on track. An outline can help a writer plan story flow, plot development, and character growth. George R. R. Martin, author of the bestselling series *A Song of Ice and Fire*, likens this approach to being an architect. Writers lay out the entire novel ahead of time, much like an architect creates a blueprint for a building. They know what each room is, where the walls are, and where the outlets are before they hammer the first nail.

Another way to create a manuscript is to simply start writing and see where it leads. Martin compares this approach to being a gardener. Writers who are gardeners dig a hole in the ground, plant a seed in the hole, and wait to see what grows. "No one is purely an architect. No one is purely a gardener in terms of writers," Martin says. "But many writers tend to one side or the other."[6]

Whichever path a writer chooses is up to them. But paying attention to formatting, style, dialogue, and flow is important. So is being patient while writing the first draft. Jane Friedman is a professor and author. She wrote a book called *The Business of Being a Writer*. "There are some writers I meet who simply

Some organizations offer classes and workshops for young writers. Young Chicago Authors (YCA), for example, hosts a summer poetry program for high school students.

YOUNG
CHICAGO
AUTHORS

ONLINE WRITING GROUPS

Many online groups help writers get in the creative groove. Critique Circle is one of the oldest and biggest groups. Participants can read and critique others' work through forums or direct messages. Scribophile is a global writing community in which writers can exchange ideas and discuss their writing portfolios. It also has a blog that offers tips from famous authors. Other writing groups include She Writes, the Next Big Writer, and Underlined. Most of these groups are free, but writers can pay a monthly or annual fee for a premium membership.

fear messing up and try to gather as much advice as possible before they even begin," Friedman said. "Unfortunately, the writing process is more or less defined by messing up and starting over. Writing is revising. . . . Creative work of any kind is going to involve countless bad ideas. It's important to work through the bad stuff to get to the good stuff."[7]

WRITING WORKSHOPS AND LITERARY ORGANIZATIONS

Unlike playing in a band or performing in a play, writing is an independent process. Some people prefer to create a book without any feedback or help from other writers. This can be helpful because it inspires focus and prevents people from copying others' ideas.

But many writers find it beneficial to be part of a writing community. People can join local or online writing groups, in which writers talk through ideas, work out storylines, and get feedback on their manuscripts. Getting feedback from others can help a writer look at their work in a new way and consider how readers will interact with it. "Collaborative workshops and writers' peer groups hadn't been invented when I was young," said legendary science fiction and fantasy author Ursula K. Le Guin. "They're a wonderful invention. They put the writer into a community of people all working at the same art, the kind of group musicians and painters and dancers have always had."[8]

> **Sound gives us clues about what is necessary and real. When you read [your work] aloud, there are parts you might skip over—you find yourself not wanting to speak them. Those are the weak parts. It's hard to find them otherwise, just reading along.[11]**
>
> ***—Jesse Ball, novelist and poet***

Writers can also connect with like-minded artists through national organizations and events. National Novel Writing Month (NaNoWriMo), held each year, is perhaps the most famous. Participants are encouraged to write a book at least 50,000 words long starting in November, completing a first draft by the end of the month.[9]

There are also plenty of opportunities for people interested in learning the craft of writing. They can apply for Master of Fine Arts (MFA) programs or sign up for online writing courses such as Gotham Writers Workshop. MFA programs typically require applicants to have an undergraduate degree in subjects such as English or writing. Most programs take between one and four years to complete.[10] MFA students may workshop their writing, experiment with genres, and work with experienced writers to develop their skills. This can be a great way for aspiring writers to develop connections with other writers and hone their craft.

Perhaps the most famous MFA writer's program is the Writers' Workshop at the University of Iowa. Founded in 1936, it is one of the hardest graduate writing schools to get into in the United States. Throughout its history, many famous writers have attended the program, including playwright Tennessee Williams, novelist Marilynne Robinson, and poet Louise Glück.

EDITING AND REVISING

For many authors, writing a book is a rewarding process. But just because the first draft is finished doesn't mean a book is ready to be self-published or sent to a publishing house. An essential step is editing and revising the book until it is the best it can be. This means proofreading, checking for grammar mistakes, and making sure there aren't any typos. The website NY Book Editors recommends software programs that help with editing. These include Grammarly, ProWritingAid, Scrivener, the Hemingway app, and even the spelling and grammar tools built into Microsoft Word.

Beyond editing for sentence structure and grammar, writers must also make sure that the book's content is readable. Traditionally, writers work with editors at publishing houses, who guide the entire editorial process. Some authors hire independent

TIRED OF TYPOS?

Some writers use online programs to help check their work for grammar or spelling errors. One common program is Grammarly, which can be used to review written documents. It scans the text and highlights each incorrect word or phrase. It also suggests synonyms in place of words that are overly complicated or used incorrectly.

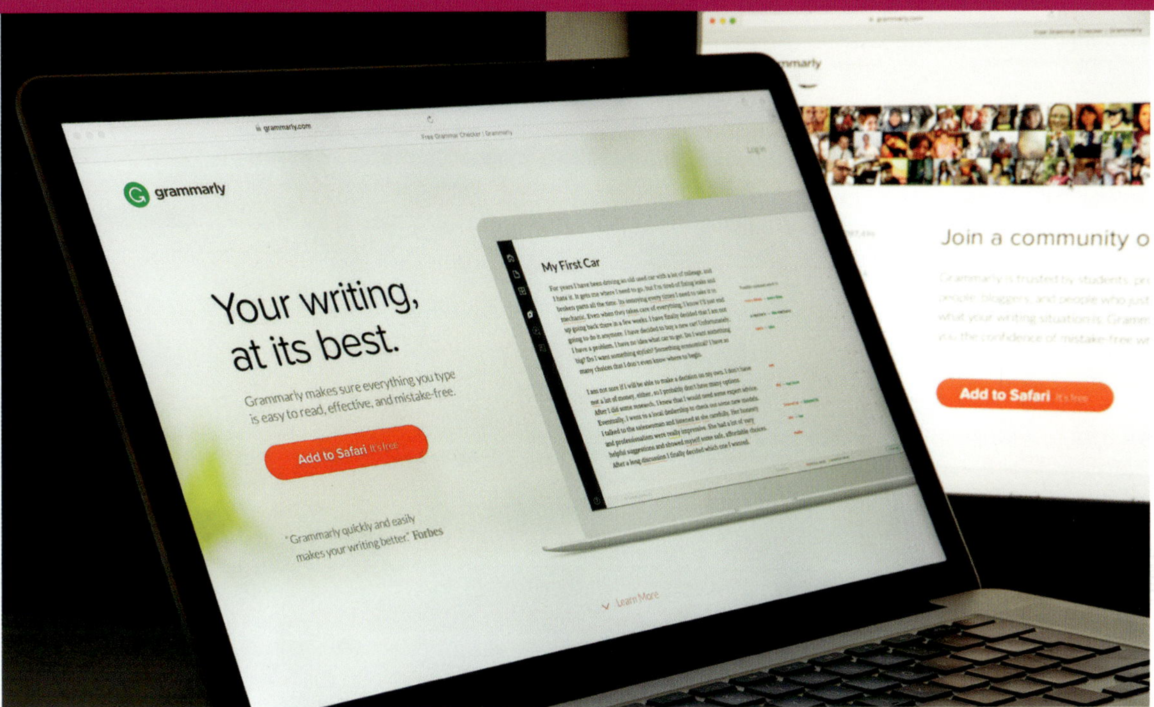

Editing tools, such as Grammarly, can help writers improve the readability and conciseness of their work. Writers can use a free version of Grammarly or pay for a premium plan.

editors or use beta readers. These people read a completed manuscript and highlight issues the author might have overlooked, such as plot holes or character inconsistencies.

Editing and revising a manuscript is a crucial step in preparing a book for publication. Some writers edit and revise their work dozens of times before getting it right. "Every book needs a LOT of editing, whether it's independently or traditionally published," says award-winning writer Jody Hedlund. "No matter how talented the author, multiple layers of editing are essential (including feedback from an objective and skilled editor)."[12]

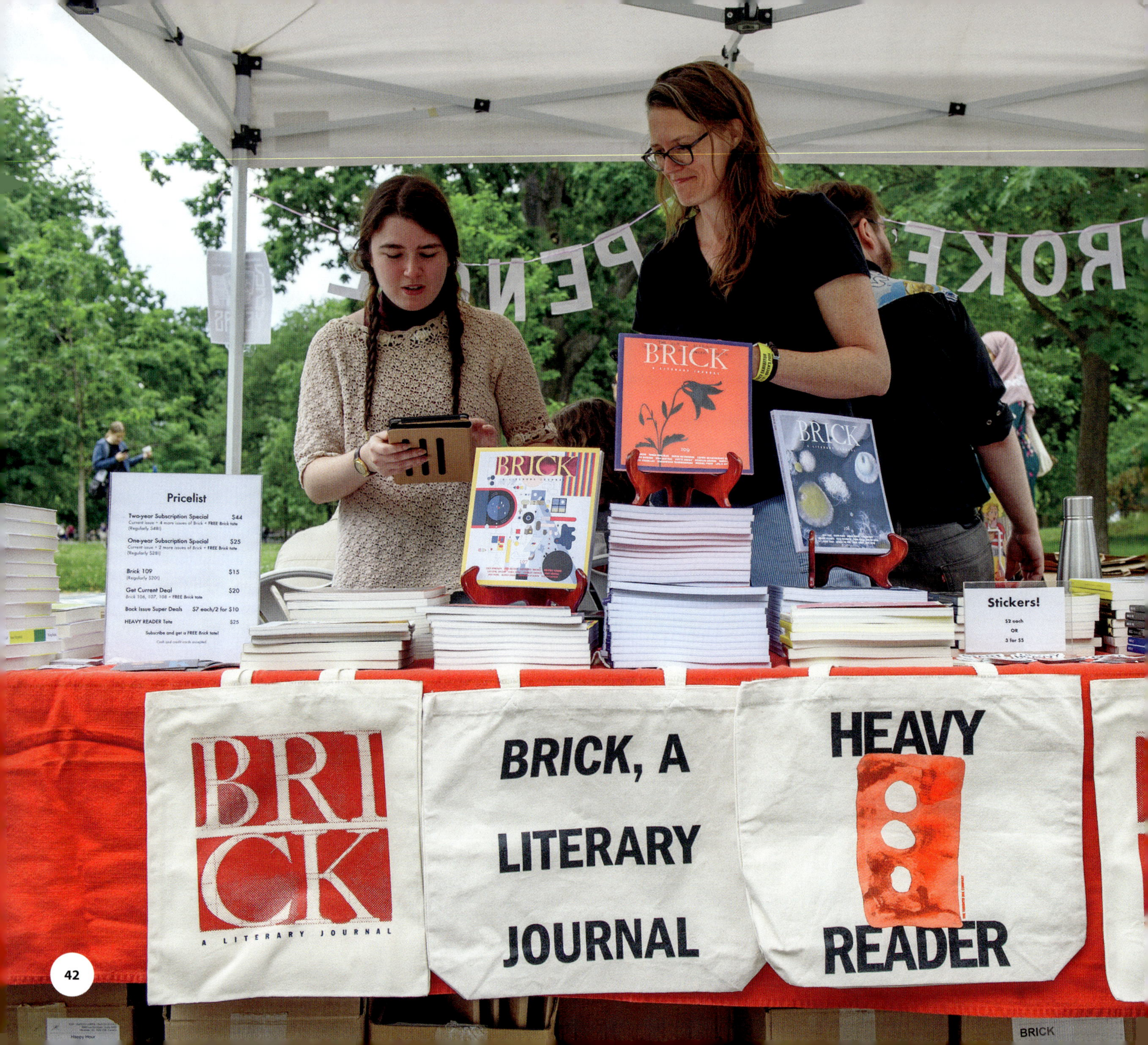
BRICK
BRICK
BRICK
Pricelist
Two-year Subscription Special $44
Current issue + 4 more issues of Brick + FREE Brick tote
(Regularly $48!)
One-year Subscription Special $25
Current issue + 2 more issues of Brick + FREE Brick tote
(Regularly $28!)
Brick 109 $15
(Regularly $20!)
Get Current Deal $20
Brick 106, 107, 108 + FREE Brick tote
Back Issue Super Deals $7 each/2 for $10
HEAVY READER Tote $25
Subscribe and get a FREE Brick tote!
Stickers!
$2 each
OR
3 for $5
BRICK
A LITERARY JOURNAL
BRICK, A
LITERARY
JOURNAL
HEAVY
READER
BRICK

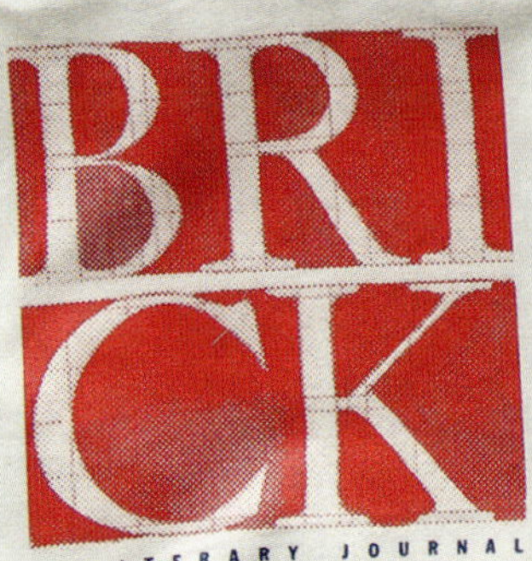

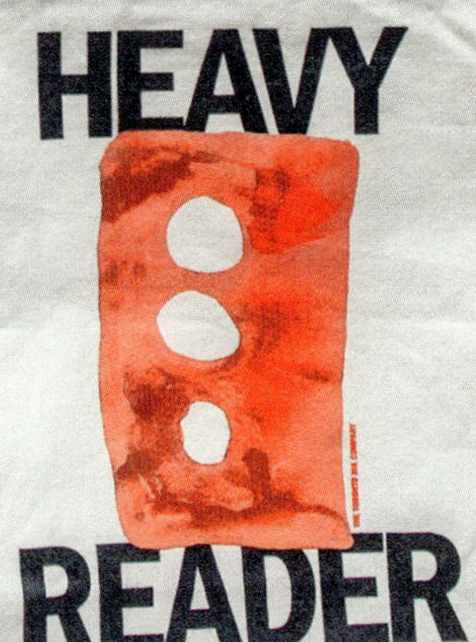

CHAPTER **FOUR**

WORKING WITH LITERARY AGENTS

Many people think aspiring authors simply submit their manuscripts to a publishing house, and then the best books get published. In the pre-internet days, this was often the case. Writers would mail a physical copy of their manuscript to a publisher's slush pile in the hopes of someone noticing it.

"The slush pile is a term that was developed in the publishing days of yore when writers would type up submissions, put them in envelopes or parcels, and mail them out to publishers and agents," says *Writer's Digest* senior editor Robert Lee Brewer. "These submissions would all arrive at their destination and be placed in a pile with other submissions."[1] These manuscripts sat in the slush pile until an editor sorted through them.

In today's publishing environment, the slush pile process still exists. But it is now in digital form. Many modern publishers use online submission programs such as Submittable. In some cases, unknown authors get discovered and published

Many writers submit their work to literary journals or magazines. Literary agents may read these journals to find potential clients.

LITERARY AGENTS VS. BOOK SCOUTS

It may sound like book scouts do the same thing as literary agents. But their jobs are different. Agents serve as mediators between publishers and authors. Book scouts don't work with authors at all. Instead, they negotiate deals between publishers in different countries. "[Book scouts are] hired by individual publishers in various countries around the world to find and recommend books for them to buy the translation rights to and publish in their own languages," says Greyhound literary agent Maria Brannan. "They also provide the same service, only with adaptation rights in mind, for film and TV clients."[4]

through the slush pile. But that is not the norm. "Some agents and editors read through their submissions daily or weekly and keep their slush piles in great shape all the time," says Brewer. "Other teams will go through submissions monthly or quarterly. Still others will do it annually, and it's possible that submissions completely fall through the cracks in other places."[2]

Most books published by traditional publishers go through an additional step before they get to the publishing house. They are vetted through literary agents. A literary agent's job is to sell a manuscript to a publisher. "An agent is a negotiator, editor, manager, mentor, friend, psychologist, fan, critic, marketeer, and impresario," says Jonny Geller, chief executive officer (CEO) of the Curtis Brown literary agency. "Most of all a connector. Someone who takes huge pleasure connecting talented people with creative collaborators and seeing them flourish."[3]

Some literary agents work alone, while others are part of a larger agency. Some of the top literary agencies in the United States include Writers House, Trident Media Group, and Folio Literary Management. Agents at these companies fill many roles.

EMILY VAN BEEK

Emily van Beek started her publishing career in the editorial department at Hyperion Books for Children in New York City. During that time, she worked with many literary agents. She eventually decided to switch her focus. She got a job as an agent at the publisher Pippin Properties and worked there for six years.

In 2023, van Beek was serving as a partner and literary agent at Folio Jr., a part of Folio Literary Management. She focuses on young adult (YA), middle grade, and picture books. Some of her award-winning clients include Jenny Han, Siobhan Vivian, Adele Griffin, Matthew Reinhart, and Sydney Smith.

Day to day, van Beek works on contracts and goes through her digital slush pile. She pitches promising manuscripts to editors at publishing houses. She also scours the internet for emerging talent looking for representation.

"I'm eager to find novels that are high concept, diverse, fantasy or magical realism, and am open to anything conceptually unique. . . . Give me something bold and fresh with a voice that's impossible to put aside," van Beek says. "What I'm really looking for is the intersection between stellar writing and plot, something that leaves me puffy eyed or laughing out loud. I am looking for emotional connection, for drama, for hope."[5]

Emily van Beek has served as an agent for YA author Jenny Han. She helped secure deals for several of Han's novels, including *The Summer I Turned Pretty*.

To me, being a literary agent is the best job in the business—you get to do everything. You've got to be a person who loves talking to people, who is naturally curious and who is willing to let other people shine, without feeling diminished yourself.[6]

—Jonny Geller, CEO of literary agency Curtis Brown

They find promising new manuscripts, help authors fine-tune their work, and bargain with book publishers to get authors a good sale price. Most agents focus on a particular genre or subject.

Bill Clegg of the Clegg Agency is one of the country's top literary agents. He has represented many authors, including Lauren Groff, Tao Lin, Nick Flynn, and Ottessa Moshfegh. He handles memoir, literary fiction, narrative nonfiction, and poetry. Literary agent Emily van Beek works for Folio Literary Management, where she handles young adult (YA) submissions. Her clients include Jenny Han, Lois Lowry, and Tamora Pierce.

ACQUIRING MANUSCRIPTS

Literary agents often get hundreds of submissions every week. They sort through those submissions to find a manuscript that they think might sell. Authors send an agent their query letter and manuscript, hoping for representation. If the agent thinks the author's proposal sounds promising, they respond and agree to represent them. Literary agents may also look online for potential clients. They might read a news story or opinion article in the *New Yorker* and think the author should write an expanded piece on the topic. In this case, they'd contact the author of the article and pitch them the idea.

Literary agents can also find new book projects by posting a call for submissions on social media profiles or on websites such as Poets & Writers, Agent Query, and Duotrope. Duotrope is a subscription-based site that has a searchable database of current fiction, poetry, nonfiction, and visual art publishers and agents. It also includes a calendar of upcoming submission deadlines and a personal submission tracker.

Literary agents also hunt for new talent at writers' conferences, such as the Society of Children's Book Writers and Illustrators (SCBWI) conferences or the Association of Writers & Writing Programs (AWP) Conference. "Writers' conferences are one of the few spaces where book lovers can freely interact with each other," says writer Sean Glatch. "These conferences connect writers, editors, publishers, and agents across the writing community, and some conferences include opportunities to network and pitch your manuscript."[7]

WHAT IS A QUERY LETTER?

When authors send unsolicited manuscripts to agents, they usually attach a query letter. A query letter is similar to a cover letter for a job application. It includes information about a manuscript's major plot points, its length, who its intended readers are, and what titles it is comparable to. A good query letter also contains biographical information about the author and a few sentences about the manuscript's potential in the literary marketplace.

PERFECTING THE PRODUCT

Once a literary agent picks up a manuscript and decides to represent its author, a few things can happen. Previously, agents mostly sold manuscripts to publishers. But since the early 2000s, some agents have started doing more than that.

A literary agent might read through a manuscript and give its author suggestions about what to revise or cut. For nonfiction books, the agent might do some fact-checking. They check to see if the material is accurate or has any factual holes.

"Authors need their agent to have the expertise, experience, and instinct to tell them what to do and then they can decide whether they agree with you or not," says Geller. "My job really is to identify somebody who can write a story in a way that only that person could have written it. If I can identify that voice then I'm halfway there."[8]

MAKING THE DEAL

Once the initial editing and revising process is done, the manuscript is considered ready for sale. The biggest part of a

Many writers' conferences and book fairs have areas where writers can meet with literary agents. For instance, the Frankfurt Book Fair in Germany has a Literary Agents and Scouts Center.

LitAg
Entrance
For registered
agents only

Literary agents often advise authors about how to revise and edit their manuscripts. They may also pitch the manuscript to publishers or negotiate deals with film producers.

literary agent's job is to act as a mediator between the author and publisher. This is an important role. While some publishers accept unsolicited submissions from authors, many will accept manuscripts only through agents. "Literary agents are a great tool for filtering out unwanted manuscripts, so when an agent approaches a book publisher with a new manuscript, that publisher knows the story has been vetted and approved by someone with a legitimate opinion," explains Glatch.[9]

In terms of day-to-day tasks, literary agents juggle numerous responsibilities. They contact acquiring editors, hoping to find a good fit for their clients' manuscripts.

They attend trade shows such as the Bologna Children's Book Fair. They meet with editors to discuss potential projects. When a publisher shows interest in a manuscript, agents help negotiate the best deal. This may include a book advance, or money paid to the author before the book's publication.

Because the agent gets a cut from the sale—the industry standard is a 15 percent commission on all book advances and royalties, and a 20 percent commission on overseas sales—it is in their best interest to get the highest price possible.[10] Sometimes this results in a bidding war. This is a phenomenon that happens when multiple publishers compete over the right to acquire a book. Usually the publisher that makes the highest bid wins the bidding war.

> **"A literary agent helps writers. That is fundamentally it. An agent helps you refine your work, edit your materials, match you with an editor, negotiate your deal, answer your questions, hold your hand, explain things to you, advocate for you, be honest with you, tell you the hard truth, hold you accountable.[11]"**
>
> ***—Kate McKean, literary agent***

After a publisher agrees to buy a manuscript, the agent helps the author negotiate a contract. A typical book deal contract lays out royalties and the amount of the advance. The contract also establishes a timeline for any revisions that the publisher wants the author to make.

A PRESIDENTIAL BIDDING WAR

In February 2017, one of the largest literary bidding wars took place over yet-to-be-published books by two of the most famous people in the world at the time: Barack and Michelle Obama. Multiple publishers, including HarperCollins, Macmillan, and Simon & Schuster, vied for the right to publish two books by the couple. In the end, the Crown imprint of Penguin Random House was the winner. It paid around $65 million for the sale.[13]

Literary agents are a great way for authors to have an advocate in their corner. But some authors have had bad experiences with agents who have poor track records of selling books to publishers. Many publishing professionals advise writers who are just starting out in the business to do ample research before deciding what's best for their project.

"I love literary agents. They can be a wonderful boon to a writer's project and writing career," says Brewer. "But they're not right for every project. My advice—once you've finished your manuscript or book proposal—is to think about which publisher(s) are a good fit for your book. Then, check out their submission guidelines to see if you need a literary agent to get in the door."[12]

Literary agent Felicity Blunt has worked with many well-known authors. She represented author Bonnie Garmus, who wrote the bestselling 2022 novel *Lessons in Chemistry*.

SCHOLASTIC
SCHOLASTIC

TRADITIONAL PUBLISHING HOUSES

Most people know that publishing houses publish books. But they may not know all the processes involved in publishing. Publishing houses, including some smaller presses, are vast companies with departments full of people who handle different aspects of book creation.

If an author signs with a particular publishing house, the publisher's employees take care of everything. This includes editing the manuscript, creating marketing materials for the book, and figuring out how many copies to print. The entire process, from acquisition to publication, can take a year or more.

Joel Richardson is a publisher at Penguin Random House. "Publishing is a team effort. It relies on such a range of different expertise," he says. "The best book in the world might never be read if it didn't have a great cover to make you want to pick it up, a skilled publicist to make sure you know about it, and a brilliant distribution team working tirelessly to ensure that the book is actually there to buy, whether on a shelf in a bookshop, or in the warehouse of an online retailer."[1]

Many big-name publishing companies have multiple locations around the world. Scholastic has branches in the United States, Canada, the United Kingdom, and parts of Southeast Asia.

PUBLISHING HOUSES VS. SMALL PRESSES

Many types of companies publish books, from large publishing houses to smaller presses. The five major US publishing houses are often called the "Big Five." They are the companies Penguin Random House, Macmillan, Simon & Schuster, Hachette Book Group, and HarperCollins.

Each company has smaller publishers that create different types of books. For example, Penguin Random House has eight publishing houses. These include Dorling Kindersley (DK), Penguin Publishing Group, Penguin Young Readers, Random House Children's, and Knopf Doubleday Publishing Group.

Below publishers, there are even smaller department breakdowns called imprints. Penguin Young Readers has 14 imprints, including Dial Books for Young Readers, Viking Children's Books, and Philomel. "The easiest way to think of any imprint is that it has a specific brand identity within the publishing world, in terms of the kinds of books they publish," says Richardson.[2]

Independent, or indie, presses have fewer staff members and lower budgets than large publishing houses. They also typically publish fewer books. Indie presses don't have all the star power of the Big Five. But they still handle many of the same processes as their larger counterparts.

Penguin Random House has more than 300 imprints. Each imprint has a unique logo often shown on book spines. The Penguin Classics imprint is famous for its penguin logo.

One well-known indie press is Graywolf Press, which is located in Minneapolis, Minnesota. It publishes fiction, nonfiction, poetry, and short stories. It releases about 35 titles every year. In 2017, Graywolf Press published Carmen Maria Machado's *Her Body and Other Parties*, which was a National Book Award Finalist. Soho Press, located in New York City, is another indie press. It produces about 90 books a year. It's known for its Soho Crime thriller imprint. It's also known for the imprint Soho Teen, which publishes YA fiction.[3]

> **In re-organizing the priorities of book publishing—by inventing new models rather than trying to repeat past success, by valuing ingenuity over magnitude, by thinking of sales as a way to make great books possible rather than the point—indie presses aren't just becoming the places where the best books are published; they're already there.[5]**
>
> ***—Nathan Scott McNamara, writer, on indie presses***

THE EDITORIAL PROCESS

Once a manuscript is acquired by a publishing house, its first stop is the editorial department. The managing editorial team takes care of the overall publishing schedule from start to finish. This includes maintaining and modifying the production schedule and shepherding book jackets and manuscripts from one department to another.

An editor is assigned to the manuscript. The editor works one-on-one with the author to turn the manuscript into a finished book. This means going through various editorial stages, including developmental editing to improve the book's overall structure and flow.

"For a developmental edit, I look at some of the larger questions," says Harlequin editor Mary-Theresa Hussey. "Why are the characters behaving as they do? What are their motivations? Do these scenes add to the overall story? What is your underlying theme, and how does it change?"[4]

Next the manuscript undergoes line editing, which involves doing a sentence-by-sentence analysis of the text.

It may also need to go through a copy edit, spell-check, and fact-check. Chersti Nieveen is a YA author and freelance editor. She says, "A copy editor's job is to bring the author's completed manuscript to a more professional level. A copy edit helps create the most readable version of your book, improving clarity, coherency, consistency, and correctness."[6]

Following the copy edit, the manuscript is proofread. At this stage, staff members or freelance proofreaders check the text for style inconsistencies or layout issues. For example, the proofreader might flag a word that is spelled incorrectly.

BOOK DESIGN AND PRODUCTION

After a manuscript is fully edited, it is ready to head to the next stage of the process: design and production. These in-house departments take care of turning the manuscript into a physical book. Staff members in the art division may hire design agencies, freelancers, photographers, artists, illustrators, and graphic designers to create the book's elements, such as a jacket, cover,

SENSITIVITY READERS

An increasingly important step in a publisher's editorial process is to hire in-house or freelance sensitivity readers. These people read a manuscript to determine whether its content might be considered offensive, stereotypical, cliché, or inaccurate. Sensitivity readers have usually had experiences that the author hasn't. Sometimes they are people of an identity that the author is trying to portray in the book. For example, sensitivity readers scan for inauthentic depictions of race, disability, religion, mental illness, gender fluidity, or sexual assault.

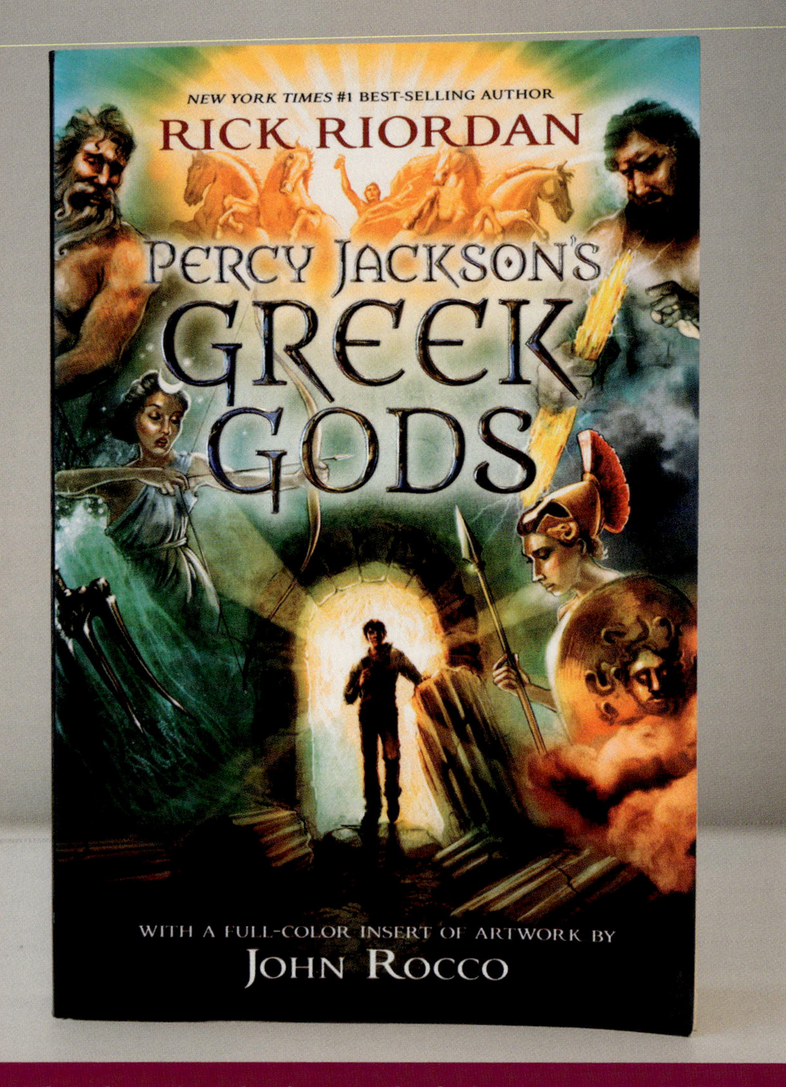

When designing a book cover, the design team must consider elements such as fonts and colors. For some books, such as Rick Riordan's *Percy Jackson* series, designers work with an illustrator to develop cover art.

and how chapter headings look on the page. The staff may use graphic design software such as Adobe InDesign or Photoshop. They work with the editorial and marketing teams to make sure the messaging and packaging for the book is consistent across all fronts.

The production group oversees the prepress and book manufacturing process. Prepress refers to the stage when a book is in digital layout form but not yet ready to be printed. This team helps transition a manuscript to its final form as a bound book. Using graphic design software, they lay out the text and ensure there aren't any strange page breaks. They may also look for orphans and widows—single words or groups of words that sit alone at the bottom or top of a page.

CREATOR **SPOTLIGHT**

GLORY ANNE PLATA

Glory Anne Plata started her publishing career as an intern at the New Press. She rotated between the company's four major departments—editorial, publicity and marketing, subsidiary rights, and the publisher's office. She spent one month in each department. "We were able to get a feel for what really interested us," Plata said. "It was an eye-opening process."[7]

By the end of her internship, Plata knew she wanted to become a publicist. She spent many years climbing the ladder. By 2023, she had become the assistant director of publicity at Riverhead Books, an imprint of Penguin Random House.

Every day, Plata sends out hundreds of pitch emails to media outlets, trying to get coverage for Riverhead's books. She writes press materials, organizes author tours, and sets up bookstore events. She even advises authors on things such as using social media, staying confident at speaking engagements, and handling negative reviews of their books.

"My boss used to tell me that a publicist's job is comprised of a variety of roles: promoter, scheduler, travel agent, art director, event coordinator, author therapist, and friend," Plata says. "I've come to learn that all of those things are true!"[8]

Riverhead Books is one of 20 imprints within Penguin Random House's Penguin Publishing Group. It publishes fiction and nonfiction titles.

ADVANCED READERS COPIES

The publishing industry has plenty of insider lingo. One example is the acronym ARC. This stands for "advanced readers copy." This is an early version of the book that is not yet finalized. The production department creates ARCs. Then the publicity department sends the ARCs out to the media so the book can be marketed and reviewed before it is officially published.

The production team works with printers and manufacturers to make sure the book is printed properly. They also keep track of the book's production budget.

PUBLICITY AND MARKETING

While these processes are underway, the marketing and publicity teams start generating buzz for the book. The marketing department puts together campaigns, such as bookstore displays, and secures advertising in newspapers, magazines, online publications, and radio stations. Claire Morrison was formerly DK's deputy marketing director. "At DK, we have a digital marketing manager and digital marketing executive who run all our social media and email campaigns, while me and the rest of the team run campaigns booking digital advertising, coming up with social strategies for our individual titles and advertising with influencers," she said.[9]

In the publicity department, publicists write press releases and create press kits for the book. They pitch editors and talent bookers at newspapers, magazines, television and radio stations, and websites or blogs. They try to persuade these outlets to review the book or write an article about it. They may also set up publicity events, such as interviews with the book's author or illustrator.

Publicists may create social media campaigns and plan author tours, which might include book signings at bookstores, libraries, and schools. Some author tours include speaking events at conferences and literary festivals around the world. Not every author gets to do a book tour—those are usually reserved for the publisher's biggest titles of the season. But even if a book isn't given a large marketing budget, some publicists will consider working with authors to plan local events.

SALES AND DISTRIBUTION

The sales and distribution divisions manage a publishing house's relationship with booksellers across the globe. The sales team makes sure books are available to readers

As part of a book's publicity campaign, an author may speak about the book at literary events. Author Rick Riordan has promoted his books at events such as the Miami Book Fair.

Some companies, such as the nonprofit Small Press Distribution, work specifically with independent publishing houses.

in every place where books are sold. This includes bookstores, supermarkets, malls, and online platforms. Sales representatives travel around their geographical area and meet with booksellers. The representatives pitch the best books for sellers to feature in their stores that month.

Working alongside the sales department, the operations team decides how many books to print or reprint if sales of the book are strong. The fulfillment team works with warehouses to make sure they receive, store, pack, and ship out books to customers. On average, Penguin Random House's fulfillment centers ship out more than 1.8 million books a day to readers around the world.[10]

Finally, multiple departments ensure that print books are transformed into audiobooks and e-books correctly. The audio team, digital production team, and development team are usually involved in this step. The digital production team makes sure the layout looks clean and the text is easily readable. Any photographs or illustrations must be transferred properly to a digital format.

The team must also make sure some e-books have the correct video and audio clips. If a book needs an audiobook version, the team works on securing rights, managing the production schedule, and casting voiceover actors to read the text. The departments work together to make sure each book is well-packaged, marketed, and publicized when it is released.

FROM BOOK TO MOVIE

From Alice Walker's *The Color Purple* to Louisa May Alcott's *Little Women*, dozens of books are made into movies or TV shows every year. When someone wants to make a book into a movie or show, a publisher's subsidiary rights department handles the contracts and licensing involved. The book adaptation process starts with an option agreement. This is when an author sells a producer, production company, or screenwriter the temporary but exclusive right to adapt the book for the screen.

reedsy

Connect Blog Apps Tools

Where beautiful adventure books are made

Meet the editor, designer or marketer who can help bring your book to life.

Enter your email... Get started

Sign up with facebook or  Sign in with Google

SELF-PUBLISHING BOOKS

When people think about creating a book, they often imagine people such as Stephen King or J. K. Rowling—writers who had recently started writing, got picked up by publishers, and soon had their books on shelves. But that's not the only way to get a book published.

Some writers choose to tackle the publishing process themselves. Andy Weir, for example, self-published his novel *The Martian* before it was picked up by Penguin Random House. Many authors who self-publish like the freedom that comes with being able to do what they want, how they want, when they want.

Fantasy author Jenna Moreci enjoys the creative power of self-publishing. "I don't have anyone giving me deadlines; I give myself deadlines," she says. "I don't have anyone telling me how I need to write my story for it to be marketable. I get to decide how I write my story. No one gets to have creative control over me."[1]

There are three main ways to self-publish a book. The first is to self-publish by paying a service company to help with the layout and printing. The second is

Some self-publishing service companies, such as Reedsy, offer editing and formatting tools. Authors can also use the platform to connect with professional proofreaders and book designers.

THE COST OF SELF-PUBLISHING SERVICES

Many authors who self-publish their work hire freelancers through a service company. The freelancers assist with a range of editorial, marketing, and design tasks. The cost of these jobs varies depending on the freelancer's location and skill level, along with the length of the project. According to Reedsy, the average price for developmental editing a self-published 60,000-word nonfiction book in 2023 was $2,178. It was $1,506 for copy editing, $948 for proofreading, $700 for cover design, and between $250 and $750 for formatting.[3]

to do the whole process independently by hiring freelancers to handle the tasks that a publishing house would normally do. The third is to work with a hybrid publisher that allows writers to pick and choose what they need help with and what they want to do themselves. There are benefits and drawbacks to each method. For example, self-published books usually aren't stocked in physical bookstores.

SELF-PUBLISHING SERVICE COMPANIES

Out of the three self-publishing options, hiring a service company involves the least work. Jane Friedman calls it the "write a check and make the headache go away" method of self-publishing. "If you have more money than time, and have no interest in being a full-time career author, this may best serve your needs," she says.[2]

But there are a few downsides to this arrangement. Self-publishing service companies such as Reedsy or BookBaby usually charge an up-front fee or connect writers to freelancers who charge fees. This can cost as little as $500 or as much as $20,000.

ANDY WEIR

Andy Weir first started writing the manuscript for his novel *The Martian* in 2009. He published it as a serial on his website. He released the book one chapter at a time. "I slowly accumulated this core group of about 3,000 readers over ten years of posting stuff to my website," Weir said.[4]

During this time, Weir's readers said *The Martian* was a headache to read on their computer screens. To make it easier to read, Weir self-published the book on Kindle in 2012. "By December it was on the top sellers list," he recalls. "I wanted to put it up for free, but it wouldn't let me. So, it was like 99 cents, which is the minimum they'd allow."[5]

The Martian went viral when it was released in 2012. It sold 35,000 copies in three months. Podium, a small Canadian audiobook company, bought the rights to the book and made it into an audiobook.[6]

Then Penguin Random House got wind of Weir's success and bought the book. In 2014, they republished it in hardcover. *The Martian* appeared on all the bestseller lists, and it was even made into a blockbuster movie starring Matt Damon.

In 2019, Andy Weir attended the Silicon Valley Comic Con in San Jose, California.

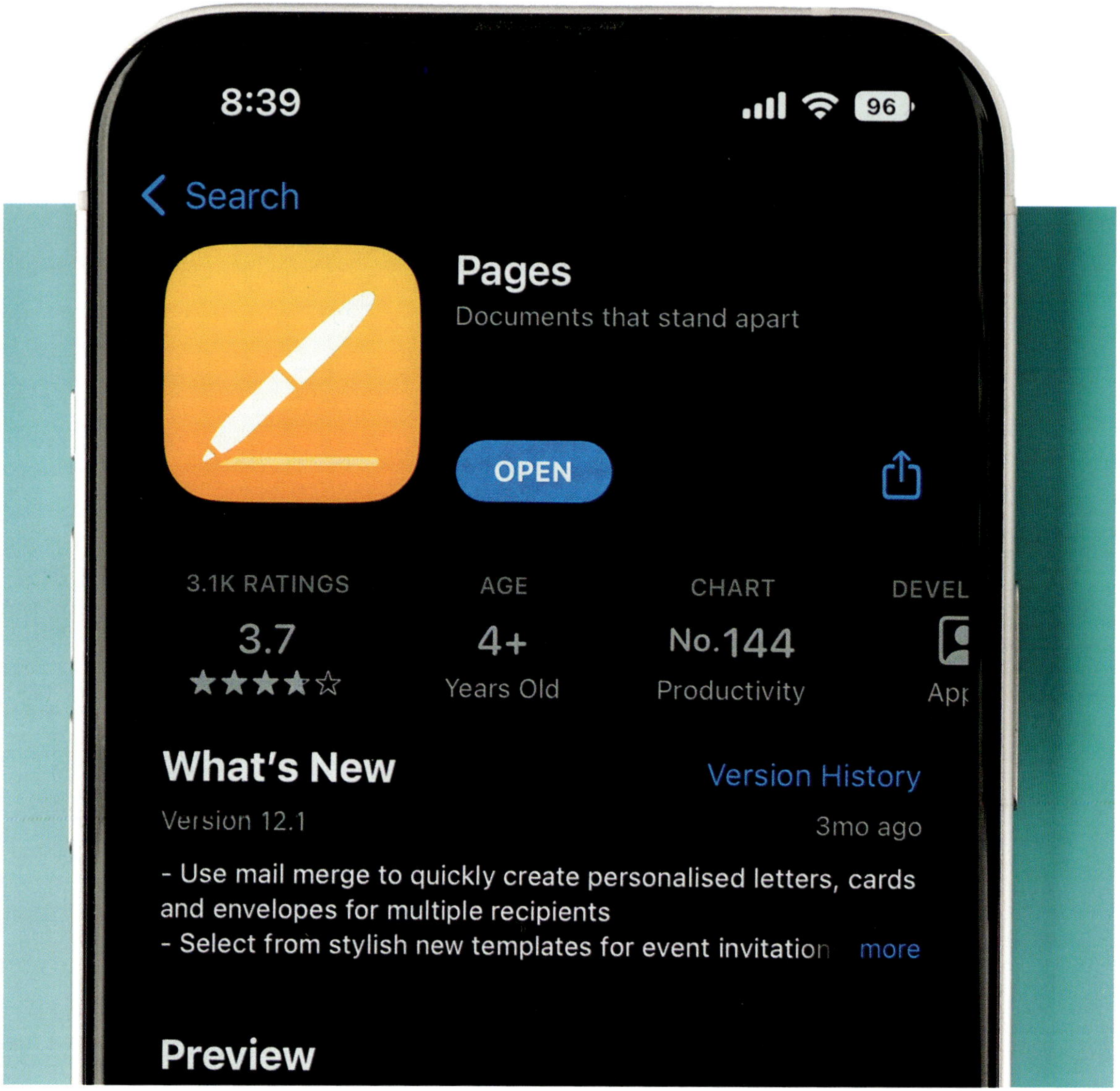

Apple Pages offers a variety of interactive book templates. Users can export a book in EPUB format and then publish it directly to Apple Books.

Despite the price tag, working with self-publishing service companies can have benefits. Some services allow authors to maintain control over the creation and production of their books, including keeping all rights to their work. The service company doesn't take a percentage of the book's sales—100 percent of the profits go to the author.

These companies can also help authors who don't have a large network by finding freelancers, such as editors. Books produced by these companies are usually sold through popular online retailers. Examples include Amazon, Powell's, and Bookshop.org.

The Alliance of Independent Authors has a directory of vetted global companies that offer self-publishing services at different price levels. Authors can pick and choose what they'd like to buy. Some examples of reputable companies include Girl Friday Productions, Author Imprints, and Matador.

SELF-PUBLISHING CLASSES

Writers interested in self-publishing can take classes to learn more about it. Some local literary organizations or writing centers offer self-publishing courses. These classes are taught by experienced writers and artists. One example is the Loft Literary Center in Minneapolis, Minnesota. It hosts a variety of classes focused on many different writing and publishing topics. Several courses involve learning how to navigate the world of self-publishing.

SOLO SELF-PUBLISHING

Today, it is possible for authors to publish a book on their own, even if starting from scratch. An author going this route manages the operation from start to finish.

Even with a snappy title, a book cover with plain text on a plain background will probably get lost in a busy e-bookstore. Get readers to notice your work among the rows of competing books before they can even judge it.[9]

—J. D. Biersdorfer,* New York Times *reporter

Authors who do everything themselves keep all profits from their book sales. They retain the full rights to the material. And they can do everything on their own timeline.

"You, the author, manage the publishing process and hire the right people or services to edit, design, publish, and distribute your book," says Friedman. "Every step of the way, you decide which distributors or retailers you prefer to deal with. You retain complete and total control of all artistic and business decisions."[7]

If an author chooses solo self-publishing, it means they are responsible for any editing, formatting, and proofreading done during the final editorial stages. Authors can use computer programs such as Microsoft Word, Apple Pages, Affinity Publisher, or Adobe InDesign. "You don't need special software to write a book—pretty much any modern word-processing program will do," says *New York Times* reporter J. D. Biersdorfer. "However, your text should be as mistake-free as possible, so take full advantage of any and all proofing tools you have."[8]

In addition to editing the text, the author must design the book's cover. They can use free or inexpensive graphic design sites, such as Canva or Snappa, to make

In addition to its Kindle Direct Publishing program, Amazon has several literary imprints. Amazon Publishing has had booths at book festivals and trade shows.

THOMAS & MERCER
LAKE UNION
PUBLISHING
ROBERT DUGONI
THE EIGHTH SISTER
VICTORIA SELMAN
BLOOD FOR BLOOD
Fiona Valpy
The Beekeeper's Promise
NICK SPALDING
DRY HARD
AMANDA PROWSE
The Girl in the Corner
amazon publishing

their own covers. Authors can also hire designers from graphic design studios such as 99designs and Miblart.

Some authors use their own photographs because it's easier and cheaper than hiring a professional. "If you go the D.I.Y. route, keep a few things in mind. First, do not use someone else's copyrighted photos, illustrations, or graphics without permission," says Biersdorfer. "If you use your own images, remember that e-book covers are tiny in online stores—so make the cover legible."[10]

HYBRID PUBLISHERS

Hybrid companies mix aspects of traditional publishing and self-publishing. Some hybrid publishing companies, such as Inkshares and Unbound, provide many of the same benefits as traditional publishers. But they ask authors to crowdfund money from readers before the publisher grants a contract. Other hybrid publishers, such as Greenleaf Book Group, offer the same services as a typical self-publishing service company. But they are much more selective about which projects they undertake.

Some hybrid publishers are small indie presses with a self-publishing department. They publish books using the traditional method and the author-assisted route. Whichever method a person chooses when self-publishing their book is up to them. "A good hybrid will have some method of curating or selecting what projects to take on,"

Friedman says. "In other words: They consider the market potential of your work and its ability to succeed. If they appear to take anyone and everyone, then you're better off evaluating the best self-publishing service to use."[11]

CREATING E-BOOKS

Once a manuscript has gone through the editing, proofreading, and design processes, it is time to convert it into a digital file. EPUB is the most popular format. Reading devices from Apple, Kobo, Barnes & Noble, Sony, and Google use this format. It optimizes text to fit whatever device the reader is using. For books that contain photographs or graphics, it can embed images, videos, or audio files. It even permits the reader to bookmark and highlight text.

Most e-book retailers and distributors will accept a manuscript that is sent in as a Microsoft Word document. They can then automatically convert it into an e-book. But authors can also use tools to do the conversion themselves. Calibre is a free program that creates e-book files from a

> **"Every author should begin their writing career self-publishing, even if their dream is to be with a large publisher. . . . The key to making it as a writer is to write a lot, write great stories, publish them yourself, spend more time writing, study the industry, act like a pro, network, be nice, invest in yourself and your craft, and be patient.[12]"**
>
> ***—Hugh Howey, bestselling author***

variety of file types. Vellum is a program geared toward Mac users, while Atticus is designed for writers using a Windows PC.

E-BOOK & PRINT-ON-DEMAND RETAILERS

The last stage in self-publishing is distribution. Authors can choose to sell their book as an e-book or as a book that can be printed on demand when a sale is made. Some authors use both methods.

Authors looking to make their books as widely available as possible may choose from a few e-book retailers. These include Apple Books for Authors, Barnes & Noble Press, the Books Partner Center for Google Play Books, and Rakuten's Kobo Writing Life. The most popular is Amazon's Kindle Direct Publishing program. It produces and sells e-books and print-on-demand editions.

IngramSpark is the leading site for print-on-demand book sales outside of Amazon. Self-published authors can use both IngramSpark and Amazon to maximize sales. The process is relatively quick. As soon as a printer-ready file is uploaded

PRINT-ON-DEMAND PRICING

Using the print-on-demand method to sell self-published books has many pros and cons. The biggest benefit is that with most companies, it doesn't cost anything up front. Authors simply send in the files and wait for a sale. Once a book sells, the author pays a fee to cover the printing costs. In 2023, authors on Amazon paid $4.90 per sale. On Draft2Digital and IngramSpark, authors paid $5.60 and $5.80, respectively. Some sites, such as Bookvault and BookBaby, charge a setup fee in addition to printing costs. In 2023, BookBaby charged a $399 setup fee and $6.20 per sale.[13]

to Amazon, a book can be printed by a buyer within 48 hours. With IngramSpark, it takes around two weeks for a book to be made available once it has been uploaded to the site.[14]

Whatever the method, self-publishing has become more popular than ever before. Bookstat is a company that collects online book sales data in real time from Amazon, Apple, and Barnes & Noble. It found that 51 percent of overall e-book sales in 2022 were self-published books. That year alone, e-book sales for self-published authors totaled a whopping $874 million.[15]

CHAPTER **SEVEN**

MARKETING SELF-PUBLISHED BOOKS

Authors who publish their books through a publishing house are assisted by an army of people to market the book. But writers who self-publish must handle that on their own. Many book professionals say that knowing how to market and publicize a book is just as important as writing it.

"Learning the art of book marketing is a pursuit which can often feel like an unending demand on your limited resources," says Kindlepreneur.com host Dave Chesson. "But it's a craft we must improve over time, as well as keep up-to-date with using [the] newest book tactics. Our book marketing landscape changes, and so we must too."[1]

When marketing a self-published book, there are many things to think about. The good news is that there are many different paths for authors to take. There are also several free or inexpensive resources available. Authors can check out book promotion websites and blogs for advice. Another option is taking online marketing classes, such as those offered by Udemy. Udemy hosts courses on building a mailing

Self-published authors can market their books by hosting readings or virtual launch parties.

list, advertising on Facebook, social media marketing, and other topics. People must pay a fee to take these courses. But during sales, the courses cost as little as $10 to $15.[2]

If a full-length course seems like too much of a commitment, writers can check out YouTube channels focused on self-publishing and advice for aspiring authors. Emeka Ossai's channel and Dale L. Roberts's channel both offer self-publishing tips and tutorials. Joanna Penn hosts the YouTube channel *The Creative Penn*. It features a variety of episodes about aspects of book marketing, such as "Book Marketing Mindset, Ideas, & Ambition" and "Lessons Learned from 12 Years as an Author Entrepreneur."

> **With podcasts, you can turn your morning commute or time on the treadmill into valuable book marketing education time. I've even listened to favorites of mine while waiting in line to see the doctor.[3]**
>
> ***—Dave Chesson, Kindlepreneur.com, on book-marketing podcasts***

Podcasts are another good resource. Writers can tune in to podcasts such as *Backmatter* from Leanpub or the *Sell More Books Show*, which is hosted by book marketers Bryan Cohen and H. Claire Taylor. Dave Chesson's podcast *The Book Marketing Show* covers a wide variety of topics, including TikTok campaigns, book bloggers, and insider secrets from publishing professionals.

People can also listen to audiobooks about marketing, some of which are free on Audible. Examples of these audiobook titles include *Write. Publish. Repeat:*

JANE FRIEDMAN

Author Jane Friedman has worked in the publishing industry for more than 25 years. She started out her career at F+W Media in Cincinnati, Ohio. She climbed up the ranks at *Writer's Digest*, eventually becoming its publisher. While there, Friedman launched and artistically directed the Writer's Digest Conference and *Writer's Digest* webinar series, which both persist today.

In addition to working at *Writer's Digest*, Friedman taught as a professor of e-media at the University of Cincinnati's College-Conservatory of Music. She has spoken at hundreds of conferences around the world, including South by Southwest and BookExpo America. She's also a published author of many works of nonfiction.

Friedman's biggest claim to fame is all the work she's done to help and educate writers about the self-publishing and traditional publishing processes. Her free newsletter has more than 25,000 subscribers.[4] She's written for dozens of media outlets, including the *New York Times*, *Wired*, the *Guardian*, the *Washington Post*, and National Public Radio. She's written several books on publishing topics, including *The Business of Being a Writer* and *The Authors Guild Guide to Self-Publishing*.

Jane Friedman has written articles for many literary websites and magazines, including *Writer's Digest*. This publication has been in print since 1920.

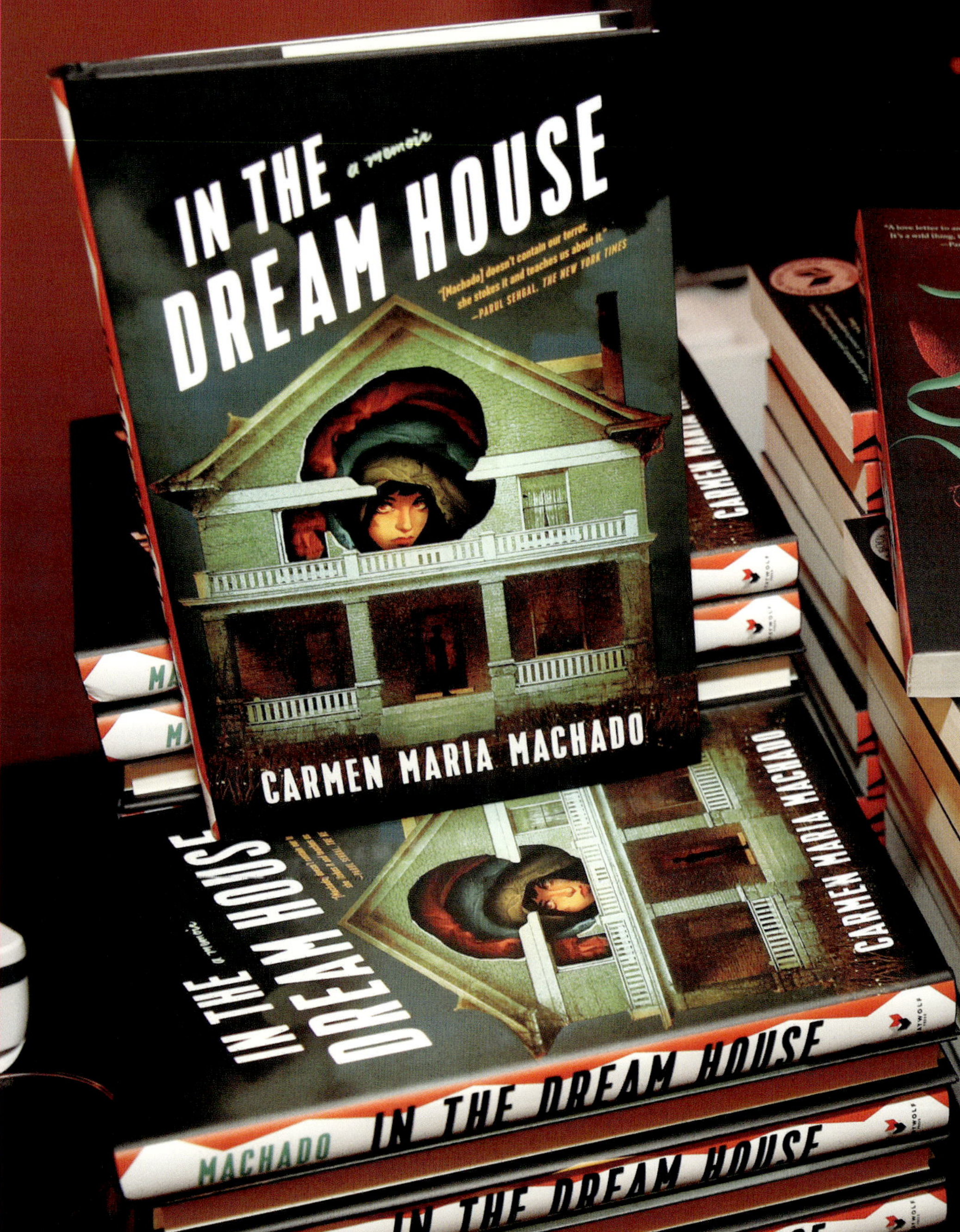
IN THE DREAM HOUSE
a memoir
"[Machado] doesn't contain our terror, she stokes it and teaches us about it."
—PARUL SEHGAL, THE NEW YORK TIMES
CARMEN MARIA MACHADO
MACHADO IN THE DREAM HOUSE
NATIONAL BOOK AWARD FINALIST
HER BODY AND OTHER PARTIES
STORIES
CARMEN MARIA MACHADO
MACHADO HER BODY AND OTHER PARTIES

The No-Luck-Required Guide to Self-Publishing Success by Johnny B. Truant and Sean Platt, *Write to Market: Deliver a Book that Sells* by Chris Fox, and *Your First 1000 Copies: The Step-by-Step Guide to Marketing Your Book* by Tim Grahl.

CREATING AN EYE-CATCHING PACKAGE

One of the main reasons that readers pick up a book at a store or click on a book while browsing online is because it has an eye-catching cover. Therefore, it is essential that the outside of a self-published book is just as dynamic as its inside. "Be sure your book cover design is spectacular. The cover is one of your most important marketing tools," says the editorial team at Gatekeeper Press. "If your cover design is just meh, do your book a big favor and hire a professional to create a captivating cover for you."[5]

After the cover, a book's plot description or summary is usually the next thing potential readers look at. A good book summary is important because it tells readers what the book is about and helps them decide if they want to read it. The editorial team at Reedsy says there are three important rules to crafting a strong book description.

The first is that it needs to hook readers with a headline. The second is that it must briefly introduce the book's plot, main idea, or thesis. The final guideline is that the summary must leave readers wanting more. Ending on a question is one way to do that. Inserting a cliffhanger in the final paragraph of the summary is another option.

Book covers may feature different fonts, illustrations, and quotes from popular writers or industry professionals.

AUTHOR PHOTOS

While the art of taking selfies has become easier than ever with smartphones, taking the perfect author photo is harder than it looks. Penguin Random House's Phil Stamper-Halpin has four tips for writers. First, they should research authors who have written similarly themed books and look at the styles of their author photos. Next, they should pay attention to lighting, making sure the photo shoot setting isn't too dark. Writers should also practice in front of a mirror before the shoot. Finally, they should take plenty of photos with different outfits and facial expressions to see which shot works best.

Writers can read the jacket copy on bestselling books to learn what kinds of summaries successfully draw in readers.

Another key element of a book package is the cover blurb. This is a quote or short passage from other writers or industry professionals in which they praise or endorse a book. Having a cover blurb from an established or well-respected author can lend a book more credibility. However, blurbs are not always necessary, especially if the author doesn't know anyone influential or recognizable.

A successful book package may also include an author photo. "Author photos are a necessary step of the publishing process," says Phil Stamper-Halpin, a senior publishing manager for Penguin Random House. "They might not come naturally to everyone, but that doesn't mean they can't be exciting. Try to relax and have fun with it!"[6]

BUILD AN ONLINE PRESENCE

Once a book's packaging is complete, the next step is creating a strong online presence for the book. Building a website that describes the book and the author's background is essential. Some authors include different sections and pages on their website to make it more interesting. One example is YA powerhouse Elizabeth Eulberg, who published *Prom & Prejudice* through Scholastic and *Past Perfect Life* through Bloomsbury YA.

Eulberg's website includes sections about her books, her background and life as an author, and any promotional events she's attending. She also has a blog and a page where educators can access discussion guides. "Your website is where you can turn readers into fans," says Chesson. "You can collect email addresses, write content, engage with readers, sell your books, and build a loyal following."[7]

In addition to making a personal website, it is important for authors to set up profiles on various book-related and publishing-related sites. Authors who sell their books on Amazon can create an "Author Central" page, which gives a writer control over their Amazon book listing page, author photo, and author biography.

> **"Now, there are many forms of traffic generation, including, but by no means limited to advertising, newsletter swaps, group promotions, and promotional sites. But you don't need to do all of them. When you're just starting out, pick one or two platforms and really get those dialed in before you start adding more to your plate.[8]"**
>
> ***—Matt Holmes, self-publishing marketing executive***

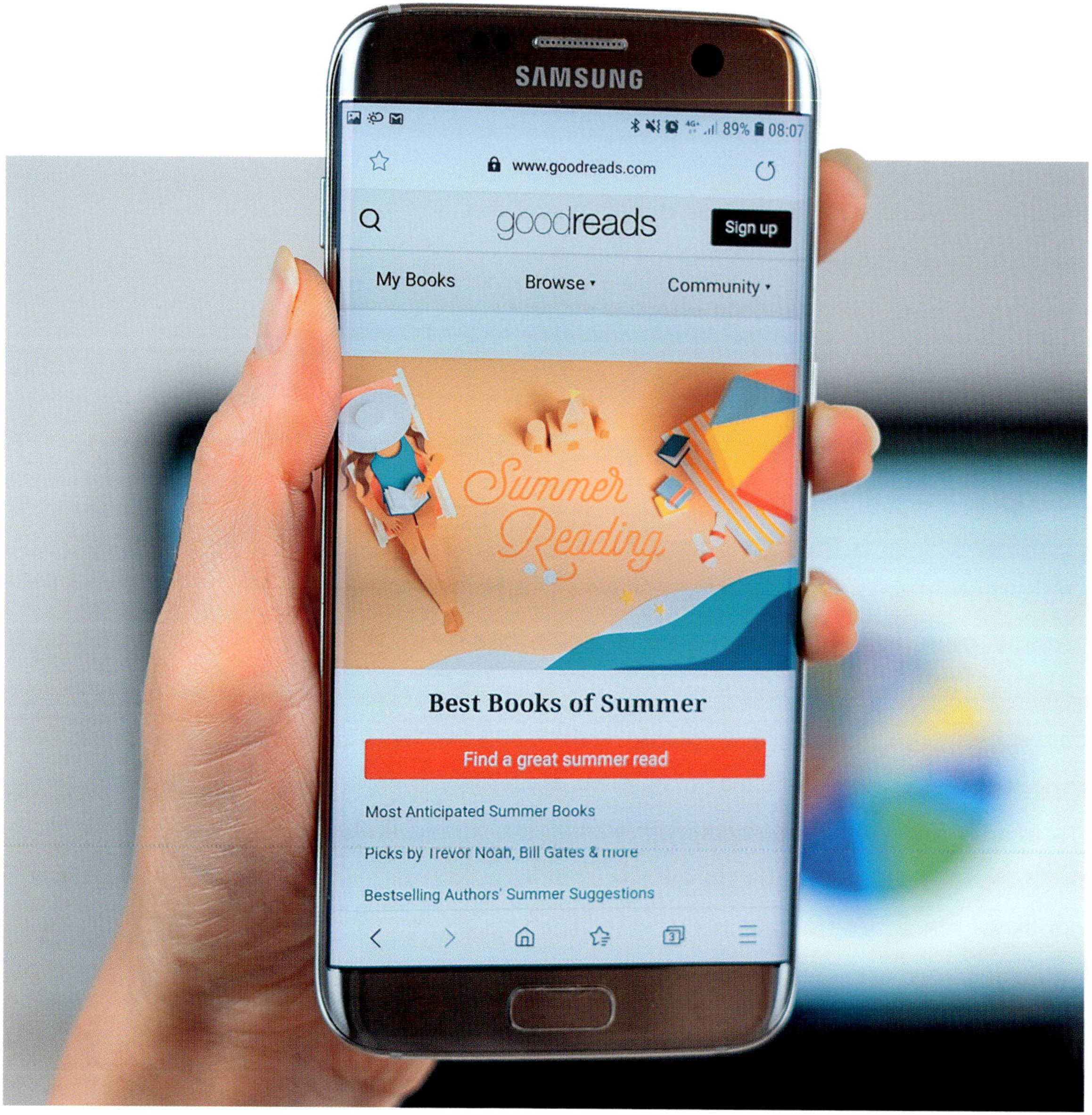

Writers can set up special author accounts on Goodreads. This allows them to interact with readers, announce upcoming projects, and promote their books.

Goodreads is another popular platform for free word-of-mouth advertising. Authors can rack up reviews from readers. They can also use the platform to run contests for book giveaways and connect with other authors writing books in similar genres.

Using social media platforms to find new readers and share news about a book is also an option for authors. Facebook, Threads, X, Instagram, TikTok, YouTube, and even LinkedIn are all helpful options. Authors can use these platforms to send out promotional blasts and find bloggers or book reviewers who might be interested in promoting the book. Social media can also be a way to connect with fans.

There are more subtle marketing techniques that shouldn't be overlooked. For example, authors can add a link to a book's sale page in an email footer. This is a great way to let people know more about the book.

USING SOCIAL MEDIA

Social media can be a useful tool for authors. Many successful writers use social media platforms such as Instagram and TikTok to engage with their fans and make announcements about upcoming releases. For example, an author might reveal their new book's cover design in an Instagram post. Another might share an unboxing video on TikTok, opening a box containing the first print copies of their novel. Some writers on social media may also post about their everyday lives, literary events such as book signings, or writing tips.

Rewards for website visitors who subscribe to an author's mailing list can increase traffic for self-published authors too. "Most authors will offer free chapters of an upcoming title, or even, in some instances, a free book or novella," says romance author

CREATIVE MARKETING IDEAS

Smith Publicity is a creative marketing team based in New Jersey. On its website, it lists ideas for marketing self-published books. Some unique ideas include making a book trailer or writing articles for publications or websites related to the book's genre. Other ideas include donating the book to places such as senior centers, children's hospitals, homeless shelters, or prisons. Authors can even try advertising on a low-cost billboard.

Camilla Monk. "If you have an online store, you can also offer a coupon for a discount on your books."[9]

GET OUT THERE

Perhaps the most effective strategy a self-published author can use to advertise an upcoming book is marketing the book in person. That means setting up local author events at bookstores, libraries, or schools. Attending book festivals and writer conferences—both as a writer and a reader—is also useful. Networking in any way possible is important.

Most of all, authors should never stop hustling. Derek Murphy is a self-publishing consultant. "Do you want to make money with your writing? Do you want to do it as a profession? Then you need to learn how to put your writing in front of readers and make them want it," he says. "Yes, the online world of book publishing is competitive and complicated, and most people have no idea what they're doing—but there's also a lot of great information out there to help you sell books if you choose to learn it."[10]

To promote their work, self-published authors can participate in literary events such as poetry slams or open mic readings. They can also collaborate with other writers.

11TH ANNUAL
CLASSIC SLAM

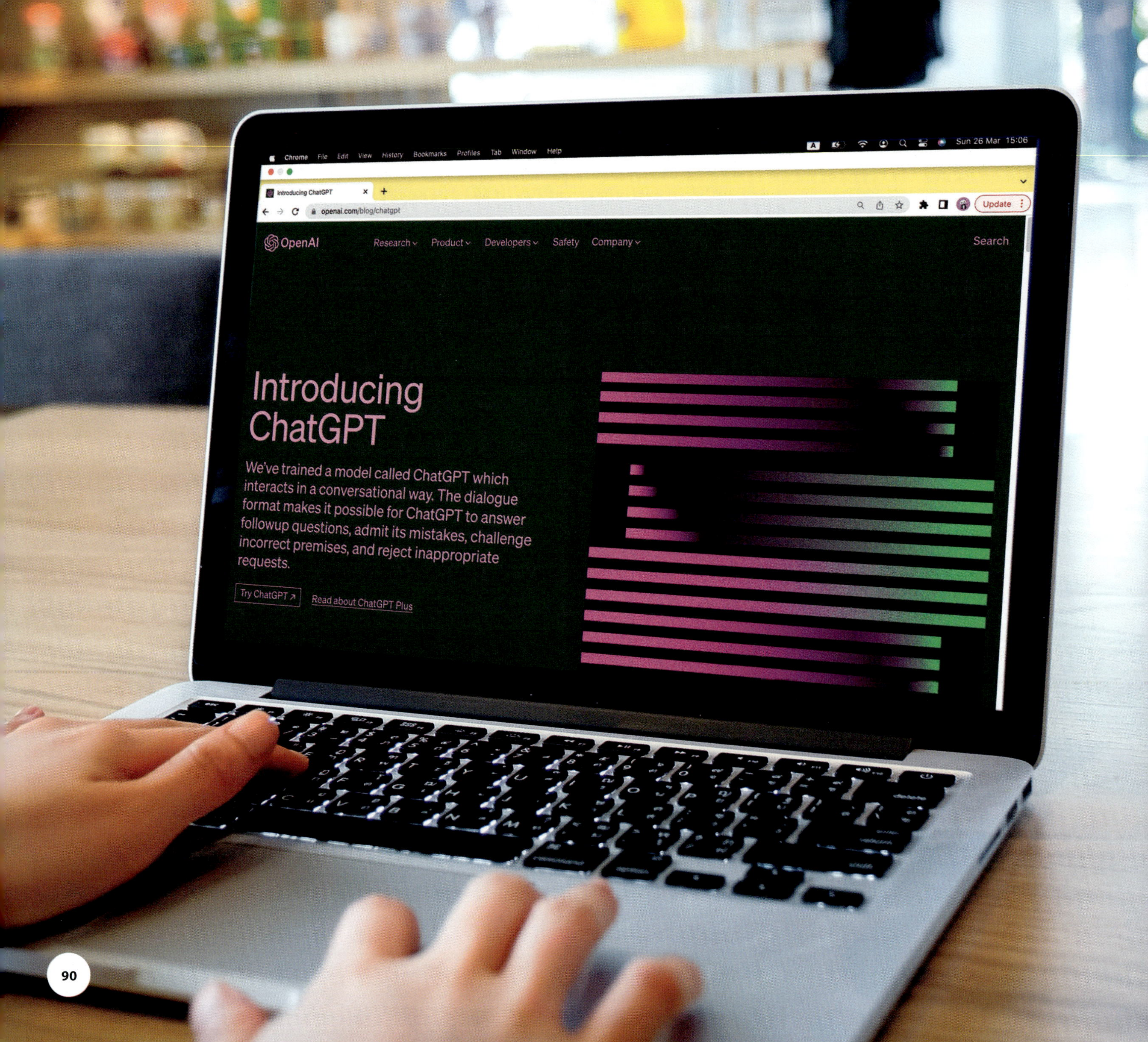
Chrome File Edit View History Bookmarks Profiles Tab Window Help
Sun 26 Mar 15:06
Introducing ChatGPT
openai.com/blog/chatgpt
Update
OpenAI
Research
Product
Developers
Safety
Company
Search
Introducing ChatGPT
We've trained a model called ChatGPT which interacts in a conversational way. The dialogue format makes it possible for ChatGPT to answer followup questions, admit its mistakes, challenge incorrect premises, and reject inappropriate requests.
Try ChatGPT ↗
Read about ChatGPT Plus

THE FUTURE OF BOOKS

Until the late 1990s, not much had changed in the art of making and publishing books. Hopeful writers submitted their work to traditional publishers. The publisher either picked their manuscripts up or rejected them. Readers bought the published book—or they didn't.

Today, more writers can get their work out into the marketplace themselves rather than going through a traditional publisher such as Simon & Schuster or HarperCollins. More books and websites are dedicated to book marketing, book production, and the writing process than ever before. The rise of e-books and digital publishing platforms has also made it easier for authors to get their work in front of readers without a traditional publisher.

But some people think the status quo of publishing is about to change in a major way. In fact, it is changing already. With new technologies such as artificial intelligence (AI)—plus an added focus on writing more diverse content—the way people create books is taking a giant leap into the future.

Many people in the publishing industry worry that tools such as ChatGPT could be used to rapidly generate books written entirely by AI. They worry this will take work away from writers.

My friends, we have a chance to become Big Publishing's worst nightmare.[1]

—Stephen King, after becoming the first major author to self-publish a book on the internet, 2000

THE RISE OF AI

In 2015, tech entrepreneurs Elon Musk, Sam Altman, Greg Brockman, and others formed OpenAI. The company's mission is to use AI in ways that benefit humanity. Since its founding, OpenAI has built many tools, including an AI image generator called DALL·E. It also created ChatGPT, an AI chatbot that can produce humanlike text based on context and past conversations. The chatbot is an example of what is called a Large Language Model (LLM).

ChatGPT was made available to the public in November 2022. Upon its release, publishing industry executives and authors began to see how the new technology and other similar machine learning (ML) models could transform the business. ML is a type of AI that enables computer software to learn how to complete tasks without being programmed every step of the way.

This type of technology could help publishers create and distribute content more efficiently and effectively. Publishers could use AI to help create and edit content, write plot summaries and pitch letters, translate books into multiple languages, and check manuscripts for plagiarism. They could even use AI to sort through their mound of unsolicited manuscripts, saving editors much time and work.

"ChatGPT will become the patron saint of the slush pile," predicts electronic publishing analyst Thad McIlroy. "Its abilities to evaluate grammar and logical expression allow it to make a once-over assessment of whether a book is (reasonably) well written. It might not spot the gems, but it will know how to separate the wheat from the chaff."[2]

But many publishers and authors worry about problems with AI technology. They argue that nonfiction books and other texts written by computers instead of humans will not be able to accurately fact-check sources. AI-created books could be full of grammatical mistakes, factual errors, or prejudicial language. "These systems can generate untruthful, biased, and otherwise toxic information," writes *New York Times* tech reporter Cade Metz. "Systems like GPT-4 get facts wrong and make up information, a phenomenon called 'hallucination.'"[3]

Another concern involves the creative aspects of writing. AI works off existing texts and rules. It does not know how to break the rules creatively or go against expectations. When used to edit an author's work, AI may also interpret stylistic choices as errors.

HOW DOES CHATGPT WORK?

A GPT is a machine learning tool that's designed based on the structure and operating power of the human brain. It works by scanning and ingesting large amounts of human-generated texts. Then, when prompted, it creates new text based on the language patterns of the data it has already digested. Based on these patterns, the tool can generate and answer questions. It constructs answers word by word, using its training data to statistically determine what would be the best next word in the response. It can also create documents in a certain style, such as a poem or news article. It can even write an entire book. Though ChatGPT may seem to improve as it "learns," its output depends on the data given to it —and the data not given to it.

DANGERS OF AI

Since its introduction in November 2022, ChatGPT has generated thousands of complaints from authors. They believe the technology and the tech industry are taking their material without asking for permission. Authors also bring up safety concerns regarding the generation of content without human oversight. For example, in 2023, several AI-generated travel guides popped up on Amazon. The guides were full of incorrect information. The problem became so severe that the New York Mycological Society issued a warning to the public to stop buying any AI-generated mushroom-foraging guides because they contained untrue—and potentially lethal—material.

It might also become harder for people to tell whether a book is written by a human or AI—or whether the material is fact or fiction. "Because these systems deliver information with what seems like complete confidence, it can be a struggle to separate truth from fiction when using them," writes Metz. "Experts are concerned that people will rely on these systems for medical advice, emotional support, and the raw information they use to make decisions."[4]

One of the biggest complaints against AI revolves around copyright infringement. In 2023, several authors sued OpenAI. The group included writers such as John Grisham, George R. R. Martin, Jonathan Franzen, David Baldacci, Elin Hilderbrand, and Jodi Picoult. They argued that the company used their books and writings to train ChatGPT without asking for their permission—and didn't offer any payment or licensing fee in return.

The lawsuit stated, "These authors' livelihoods derive from the works they create. But the Defendant's LLMs endanger fiction writers' ability to make a living in that the LLMs allow anyone to generate—automatically and freely (or very cheaply)—text that they would otherwise pay writers to create."[5] Many writers and publishing professionals continue to worry about the potential for publishing companies to replace their jobs with AI.

A MORE DIVERSE LANDSCAPE

For many years, the publishing industry was dominated by white men. This group held the majority of editing, publishing, and writing jobs. This lack of diversity was also apparent in the content of books. In 2019, the Cooperative Children's Book Center (CCBC) analyzed the children's books and YA books they received to determine their diversity statistics. Out of the 3,700 fiction books they examined, 42 percent had at least one white

George R. R. Martin was among 17 authors who filed a lawsuit against OpenAI in 2023. The Authors Guild, a group that supports writers, organized the lawsuit.

GENDER QUEER
A MEMOIR
MAIA KOBABE
Stonewall Honor Book
THE BLUEST EYE
Toni Morrison
VINTAGE
Lolita
NABOKOV
MYRACLE
l8r, g8r
THE OPPOSITE OF INNOCENT
LAWN BOY
THRIFTBOOKS
OUT OF DARKNESS
PÉREZ

main character. In contrast, only 36 percent of books featured a main character of another race.[6]

The organization Diverse BookFinder has reviewed more than 3,000 children's books since 2002. In their findings, only 29 percent of those books featured a Black character—and those books were usually about oppression and prejudice.[7] In 2020, the *New York Times* analyzed more than 7,000 books from the Big Five publishers. Ninety-five percent of those books were written by white people.[8]

But that dynamic is slowly changing. In 2020, a Black man named George Floyd was killed by a police officer in Minneapolis. His death sparked nationwide protests against systemic racism in the United States. Because of this incident and many others, long-simmering frustration about the lack of diversity and representation in the publishing industry bubbled over.

In October 2020, Hachette Book Group announced the creation of Legacy Lit, an imprint devoted to publishing books by writers of color. "There will be a huge boom of books—all of a sudden Black women are hot or urban fiction is hot—and then there will be a backslide," said Legacy Lit publisher Krishan Trotman. "That's why we need these imprints. They'll be here even after all the hoopla dies down."[9]

#PUBLISHINGPAIDME

In June 2020, author L. L. McKinney started the Twitter hashtag #PublishingPaidMe. It asked writers to share the advances they received for selling their books to publishers. As part of the discussion, a Google spreadsheet of advances circulated with about 1,200 self-reported entries. Of these, 122 authors shared that they had gotten an advance of at least $100,000. Of those authors, 78 identified as white, compared with just seven who identified as Black and two who identified as Latino.[10]

Many writers and readers are pushing for more books that tell LGBTQ+ stories, such as Maia Kobabe's graphic novel *Gender Queer*. The book has won multiple awards but has also been the target of book-banning attempts in some states.

Internal ranks at publishing houses are changing too. In 2019, nearly half of all publishing interns identified as people of color.[11] Many large publishing companies also committed to improving diversity initiatives and making their company cultures more inclusive. In a 2020 *Publisher's Weekly* report, 75 percent of people in the industry said their companies had increased diversity and inclusion efforts.[12] Examples of these efforts included hiring diversity experts and holding diversity training sessions. Several companies appointed people of color to senior positions too. Alongside Krishan Trotman, Dana Canedy at Simon & Schuster and Lisa Lucas at Pantheon and Schocken Books were two other Black women named to senior publishing jobs in 2020.

> **We're still witnessing a shift in culture that was kickstarted by a newfound transparency around wage disparity. . . . It's difficult to understand how underwater you are when you have no concept of where the surface is.[13]**
>
> ***—Leah Johnson, author, on the impact of #PublishingPaidMe***

But there's still a long way to go. A 2021 report showed that most new hires at publishing companies were still overwhelmingly white. PEN America is an organization that works to protect literature and freedom of speech. In a 2022 statement, the organization discussed the need for change in the industry.

It said, "Systemic change requires more than goodwill. It necessitates specific, far-reaching, and sustained policy revisions and company-wide commitments that outlast any single political moment and persist despite inevitable hurdles and setbacks. If publishers are the curators of our country's stories, they have an obligation to ensure that these stories reflect the breadth of our society."[14]

While the publishing world continues to change and evolve, there is still space for people to share their stories. Publishing companies are constantly adapting and bringing new books to the shelves. Meanwhile, aspiring writers have more self-publishing tools at their disposal than ever before. They can take advantage of technology and social media to build their audiences and elevate their platforms. Whether writers choose traditional publishing or self-publishing, the opportunities are endless.

Many modern authors, such as Colson Whitehead, write about the history of racism in America. Whitehead has received many awards, including the National Book Award for his novel *The Underground Railroad.*

ESSENTIAL **FACTS**

MAKING BOOKS PROFESSIONALLY

- Authors can submit unsolicited manuscripts to a publisher, who places the manuscripts in a slush pile. Acquiring editors go through the slush pile to find marketable books that might sell. A book can be acquired by an editor or publisher at one of the Big Five companies or at a smaller independent press.
- Most books published via the traditional route are brought to editors through literary agents. These people help authors sell their manuscript to a publisher, taking a cut of the sale.
- Once a manuscript is acquired by a publishing house, it goes through various stages and departments. These include the editorial, art and design, production, sales and distribution, and marketing and publicity departments.
- The publisher chooses some authors to go on tour to promote their books. During the tour, the author might take part in interviews with the media. The author might also participate in book readings and book signings at bookstores, libraries, and schools.

MAKING BOOKS INDEPENDENTLY

- Writers who choose to self-publish their book can do so in three ways: completely by themselves, by using a self-publishing service company, or by working with a hybrid publisher.
- Multiple stages are involved in self-publishing a book. Authors typically hire a freelance editor, copy editor, or proofreader. They also design a book cover. Then they convert the manuscript into a digital format so it can be uploaded to a site such as Amazon or IngramSpark. The book will be offered for sale digitally or through print-on-demand services.
- Once a self-published book is made available to the public, marketing is key to getting the word out. Some authors use social media to publicize their books through posts, contests, and giveaways.
- Self-published authors may receive a range of royalties from the sale of their books. Often, hybrid publishers take a cut. Print-on-demand companies usually take a portion of the sales in exchange for selling the book on their platform.

QUOTE

"Every author should begin their writing career self-publishing, even if their dream is to be with a large publisher. . . . The key to making it as a writer is to write a lot, write great stories, publish them yourself, spend more time writing, study the industry, act like a pro, network, be nice, invest in yourself and your craft, and be patient."

—Hugh Howey, bestselling author

GLOSSARY

chatbot
A software or computer program that is designed to generate a conversation with humans based on previously scanned text.

commission
A sum of money paid to someone after they complete a task, such as selling goods or services.

copyright
The legal means to protect a creator's work.

freelancer
A person who works by the hour, day, or project rather than working a salaried job for an employer.

influencer
A popular content creator or social media star who has a large online following and promotes products or services to their audience.

infringement
The act of breaking or violating a law or agreement; the action of limiting something.

machine learning (ML)
A branch of artificial intelligence that focuses on the use of data and algorithms to imitate the way that humans learn, gradually improving its accuracy.

mass-market
Directed toward a broad audience.

plagiarism
The act of taking someone else's work or ideas and passing them off as one's own.

royalty
A percentage of money that an author receives from a publisher based off sales terms established in the contract.

storyboard
A series of drawings or images arranged in specific order for the purpose of visualizing a story, plot, or scene.

subsidiary rights
All rights other than book publishing rights included in a book publishing contract, such as paperback rights, book club rights, and movie rights.

vet
To investigate thoroughly, as in making sure someone is suitable for a job that requires loyalty or trustworthiness.

ADDITIONAL **RESOURCES**

SELECTED BIBLIOGRAPHY

Biersdorfer, J. D. "How to Self-Publish Your E-Book." *New York Times*, 2 Aug. 2023, nytimes.com. Accessed 6 Dec. 2023.

Friedman, Jane. "Start Here: How to Self-Publish Your Book." *Jane Friedman*, 23 Aug. 2023, janefriedman.com. Accessed 6 Dec. 2023.

Glatch, Sean. "Literary Agents." *Writers.com,* 26 July 2023, writers.com. Accessed 6 Dec. 2023.

FURTHER READINGS

Jaskulka, Marie. *Making Web Content*. Abdo, 2025.

Jenkins, Jennifer. *Teen Writer's Guide: Your Road Map to Writing*. Owl Hollow, 2020.

ONLINE RESOURCES

To learn more about making books, please visit **abdobooklinks.com** or scan this QR code. These links are routinely monitored and updated to provide the most current information available.

MORE INFORMATION

For more information on this subject, contact or visit the following organizations:

Alliance of Independent Authors (ALLi)
7 Bell Yard, City of Westminster
London, WC2A 2JR, UK
allianceindependentauthors.org
ALLi is a global nonprofit organization for authors who self-publish. It hosts a daily blog, weekly live streams, and podcasts about the business of self-publishing. ALLi also has a bookstore full of self-publishing guidebooks.

Scholastic Art & Writing Awards
557 Broadway
New York, NY 10012
artandwriting.org
The Scholastic Art & Writing Awards is one of the most celebrated arts and writing contests for kids in the United States. It hosts workshops for teens and professional development courses for educators.

Writer's Digest
4665 Malsbary Rd.
Blue Ash, OH 45242
writersdigest.com
Writer's Digest is one of the longest-running publications on the craft and business of writing. It features articles about self-publishing and traditional publishing.

SOURCE NOTES

CHAPTER 1. A CREATIVE JOURNEY

1. "How to Enter." *Scholastic Art & Writing Awards*, n.d., artandwriting.org. Accessed 6 Feb. 2024.
2. "Scholastic Art & Writing Awards." *Scholastic Media Room*, n.d., mediaroom.scholastic.com. Accessed 6 Feb. 2024.
3. "How to Create an Art Portfolio." *Indeed*, 9 Dec. 2022, indeed.com. Accessed 6 Feb. 2024.
4. Rachel Nixon. "Writers: Shovel Sand So You Can Build Castles." *Medium*, 24 Aug. 2020, medium.com. Accessed 6 Feb. 2024.
5. "2019 Scholastic Art & Writing Awards National Teen Recipients Announced." *PR Newswire*, 13 Mar. 2019, prnewswire.com. Accessed 6 Feb. 2024.

CHAPTER 2. THE HISTORY OF BOOKS

1. Steven Piersanti. "The 10 Awful Truths about Book Publishing." *Berrett-Koehler Publishers*, 1 Mar. 2023, ideas.bkconnection.com. Accessed 6 Feb. 2024.
2. "Understanding Media and Culture: An Introduction to Mass Communication." *University of Minnesota Libraries Publishing*, n.d., open.lib.umn.edu. Accessed 6 Feb. 2024.
3. "Understanding Media and Culture."
4. Tatiana Schlossberg. "The State of Publishing: Literacy Rates." *McSweeney's*, 7 Feb. 2011, mcsweeneys.net. Accessed 6 Feb. 2024.
5. "Understanding Media and Culture."
6. "Understanding Media and Culture."
7. Schlossberg, "Literacy Rates."
8. Michelle Pauli. "Earliest-known Book Jacket Discovered in Bodleian Library." *Guardian*, 24 Apr. 2009, theguardian.com. Accessed 6 Feb. 2024.
9. "The Evolution of the Book." *SFBook*, n.d., sfbook.com. Accessed 6 Feb. 2024.
10. "Evolution of the Book."
11. Arvyn Cerézo. "15 Years of Kindle: A Look Back on Its Setbacks and Successes." *Book Riot,* 10 Nov. 2022, bookriot.com. Accessed 6 Feb. 2024.
12. Yashvi Peeti. "What Was the First Audiobook?" *Book Riot,* 6 Nov. 2020, bookriot.com. Accessed 6 Feb. 2024.
13. Jim Milliot. "Print Book Sales Fell 6.5% in 2022." *Publisher's Weekly*, 6 Jan. 2023, publishersweekly.com. Accessed 6 Feb. 2024.
14. Piotr Kowalczyk. "Most Interesting Quotes about Books in the Digital Age." *Ebook Friendly*, 11 Feb. 2018, ebookfriendly.com. Accessed 6 Feb. 2024.

CHAPTER 3. CREATING A MANUSCRIPT

1. "George Saunders on the Best Writing Advice He's Received." *Literary Hub*, 13 Nov. 2018, lithub.com. Accessed 6 Feb. 2024.
2. N. A. Turner. "Why Do We Write? A Love Letter to the Craft." *Medium*, 8 Oct. 2018, medium.com. Accessed 6 Feb. 2024.
3. Nathan Bransford. "How to Choose an Idea for a Novel." *Nathan Bransford*, 29 Oct. 2013, nathanbransford.com. Accessed 6 Feb. 2024.
4. Bransford, "How to Choose an Idea for a Novel."
5. Glenn Leibowitz. "50 Inspiring Quotes about Writing from the World's Greatest Authors." *Inc.*, 24 Aug. 2017, inc.com. Accessed 6 Feb. 2024.
6. George R. R. Martin. "A Winter Garden." *George R. R. Martin*, 8 July 2022, georgerrmartin.com/notablog. Accessed 6 Feb. 2024.
7. Jane Friedman. "How Can I Set Aside the Cacophony of Writing Advice and Just Write?" *Jane Friedman*, 15 Oct. 2023, janefriedman.com. Accessed 6 Feb. 2024.
8. Shaunta Grimes. "A Community of People All Working at the Same Art." *Medium*, 25 May 2019, medium.com. Accessed 6 Feb. 2024.
9. "National Novel Writing Month." *NaNoWriMo*, n.d., nanowrimo.com. Accessed 6 Feb. 2024.
10. Krysten Godfrey Maddocks. "What Is an MFA Degree? What You Need to Know." *Southern New Hampshire University*, 22 Dec. 2023, snhu.edu. Accessed 6 Feb. 2024.
11. Joe Fassler. "I Talked to 150 Writers and Here's the Best Advice They Had." *Literary Hub*, 26 Oct. 2017, lithub.com. Accessed 6 Feb. 2024.
12. Jody Hedlund. "How Much Editing Does a Book Really Need?" *Inspired by Life and Fiction*, 21 Sept. 2018, inspiredbylifeandfiction.com. Accessed 6 Feb. 2024.

CHAPTER 4. WORKING WITH LITERARY AGENTS

1. Robert Lee Brewer. "What Is the Slush Pile?" *Writer's Digest*, 22 Mar. 2021, writersdigest.com. Accessed 6 Feb. 2024.
2. Brewer, "What Is the Slush Pile?"
3. Jonny Geller. "The Life of a Literary Agent." *Curtis Brown Creative*, 16 July 2019, curtisbrowncreative.co.uk. Accessed 6 Feb. 2024.
4. Maria Brannan. "What Is a Book Scout?" *Greyhound Literary*, n.d., greyhoundliterary.co.uk. Accessed 6 Feb. 2024.
5. "Emily van Beek." *Folio Jr.*, n.d., foliojr.com. Accessed 6 Feb. 2024.
6. Geller, "The Life of a Literary Agent."
7. Sean Glatch. "Literary Agents: What They Do and How to Find One." *Writers.com*, 26 July 2023, writers.com. Accessed 6 Feb. 2024.
8. Geller, "The Life of a Literary Agent."
9. Glatch, "Literary Agents."
10. Glatch, "Literary Agents."
11. Kate McKean. "What Does an Agent Do?" *Agents and Books*, 5 Apr. 2022, katemckean.substack.com. Accessed 6 Feb. 2024.
12. Robert Lee Brewer. "Do Writers Need Literary Agents?" *Writer's Digest*, 24 Mar. 2020, writersdigest.com. Accessed 6 Feb. 2024.
13. Laura Miller. "Just How Outrageous Is the Obamas' Alleged $65 Million Book Deal?" *Slate*, 2 Mar. 2017, slate.com. Accessed 6 Feb. 2024.

CHAPTER 5. TRADITIONAL PUBLISHING HOUSES

1. "What Does a Publisher Do?" *Penguin*, n.d., penguin.co.uk. Accessed 6 Feb. 2024.
2. "What Does a Publisher Do?"
3. "Best Independent Publishers." *Reedsy*, n.d., blog.reedsy.com. Accessed 6 Feb. 2024.
4. "Types of Editing: An Inside Look at What Editors Do." *Reedsy*, n.d., blog.reedsy.com. Accessed 6 Feb. 2024.
5. Nathan Scott McNamara. "American Literature Needs Indie Presses." *Atlantic*, 17 July 2016, theatlantic.com. Accessed 6 Feb. 2024.
6. "Types of Editing."
7. "The BW Insider Series: Part 5." *Banana Writers*, n.d., bananawriters.com. Accessed 6 Feb. 2024.
8. "BW Insider Series."
9. "Interview with Claire Morrison, Deputy Marketing Director, DK." *Book Machine*, 27 Nov. 2018, bookmachine.org. Accessed 6 Feb. 2024.
10. "Department Guide." *Penguin Random House Careers*, n.d., careers.penguinrandomhouse.com. Accessed 6 Feb. 2024.

CHAPTER 6. SELF-PUBLISHING BOOKS

1. Bella Rose Pope. "Interview with Full Time Self-Published Author Jenna Moreci," *Self-Publishing School*, 23 Oct. 2018, self-publishing school.com. Accessed 6 Feb. 2024.
2. Jane Friedman. "Start Here: How to Self-Publish Your Book." *Jane Friedman*, 3 Dec. 2023, janefriedman.com. Accessed 6 Feb. 2024.
3. Lissie Kidd. "Is Self-Publishing or Traditional Publishing More Profitable?" *Forbes*, 15 May 2023, forbes.com. Accessed 6 Feb. 2024.
4. Sheryl Garratt. "Andy Weir on Writing an Accidental Best-Seller." *Creative Life*, 26 Aug. 2016, thecreativelife.net. Accessed 6 Feb. 2024
5. Garratt, "Andy Weir."
6. Rebecca Ford. "How a 99-Cent Novel Spawned 'The Martian.'" *Hollywood Reporter*, 24 Nov. 2015, hollywoodreporter.com. Accessed 6 Feb. 2024.
7. Friedman, "How to Self-Publish Your Book."
8. J. D. Biersdorfer. "How to Self-Publish Your E-Book." *New York Times*, 2 Aug. 2023, nytimes.com. Accessed 6 Feb. 2024.
9. Biersdorfer, "How to Self-Publish Your E-Book."
10. Biersdorfer, "How to Self-Publish Your E-Book."
11. Jane Friedman. "What Is a Hybrid Publisher?" *Jane Friedman*, 31 Oct. 2023, janefriedman.com. Accessed 6 Feb. 2024.
12. "Inspiring Quotes about Self-Publishing." *3 Penny Publishing*, Oct. 2023, 3pennypublishing.com. Accessed 6 Feb. 2024.
13. "Print on Demand Books: The 6 Best Services in 2024." *Reedsy Blog*, 30 Jan. 2023, blog.reedsy.com. Accessed 6 Feb. 2024.
14. Friedman, "How to Self-Publish Your Book."
15. Jim Milliot. "Self-Publishing Is Thriving, according to Bowker Report." *Publisher's Weekly*, 17 Feb. 2023, publishersweekly.com. Accessed 6 Feb. 2024.

CHAPTER 7. MARKETING SELF-PUBLISHED BOOKS

1. Dave Chesson. "4 Affordable Ways to Master Book Marketing." *Jane Friedman*, 29 Jan. 2018, janefriedman.com. Accessed 6 Feb. 2024.
2. Chesson, "Ways to Master Book Marketing."
3. Chesson, "Ways to Master Book Marketing."
4. Jane Friedman. "About Jane Friedman." *Jane Friedman*, n.d., janefriedman.com. Accessed 6 Feb. 2024.
5. "How to Market a Self-Published Book." *Gatekeeper Press*, 2 Mar. 2022, gatekeeperpress.com. Accessed 6 Feb. 2024.
6. Phil Stamper-Halpin. "Five Tips on Taking a Good Author Photo." *Penguin Random House News for Authors*, Feb. 2019, authornews.penguinrandomhouse.com. Accessed 6 Feb. 2024.
7. Dave Chesson. "Book Marketing 101." *Kindlepreneur*, 27 June 2023, kindlepreneur.com. Accessed 6 Feb. 2024.
8. Matt Holmes. "4 Pillars of Book Marketing, or How to Sell More Books in Less Time." *Jane Friedman*, 5 Apr. 2023, janefriedman.com. Accessed 6 Feb. 2024.
9. Camilla Monk. "8 Tips for Authors to Boost Their Homepage." *Jane Friedman*, 18 July 2023, janefriedman.com. Accessed 6 Feb. 2024.
10. Derek Murphy. "8 Lies Authors Tell Themselves about Book Marketing That I'm Sick of Hearing." *Creativindie*, n.d., creativindie.com. Accessed 6 Feb. 2024.

CHAPTER 8. THE FUTURE OF BOOKS

1. Jamie FitzGerald. "Notable Moments in Self-Publishing History: A Timeline." *Poets & Writers*, November/December 2013, pw.org. Accessed 6 Feb. 2024.
2. Thad McIlroy. "AI Is about to Turn Book Publishing Upside-Down." *Publisher's Weekly*, 2 June 2023, publishersweekly.com. Accessed 6 Feb. 2024.
3. Cade Metz. "What Exactly Are the Dangers Posed by A.I.?" *New York Times*, 7 May 2023, nytimes.com. Accessed 6 Feb. 2024.
4. Metz, "What Exactly Are the Dangers Posed by A.I.?"
5. Emilia David. "George R. R. Martin and Other Authors Sue OpenAI for Copyright Infringement." *Verge*, 20 Sept. 2023, theverge.com. Accessed 6 Feb. 2024.
6. Josh Howarth. "11 Top Publishing Trends (2024–2026)." *Exploding Topics*, 8 Jan. 2024, explodingtopics.com. Accessed 6 Feb. 2024.
7. Howarth, "11 Top Publishing Trends."
8. Richard Jean So and Gus Wezerek. "Just How White Is the Book Industry?" *New York Times*, 11 Dec. 2020, nytimes.com. Accessed 6 Feb. 2024.
9. So and Wezerek, "Just How White Is the Book Industry?"
10. James Tager and Clarisse Rosaz Shariyf. "Reading Between the Lines: Race, Equity, and Book Publishing." *PEN America*, 17 Oct. 2022, pen.org. Accessed 6 Feb. 2024.
11. So and Wezerek, "Just How White Is the Book Industry?"
12. Tager and Shariyf, "Race, Equity, and Book Publishing."
13. Tager and Shariyf, "Race, Equity, and Book Publishing."
14. Tager and Shariyf, "Race, Equity, and Book Publishing."

INDEX

ABOUT THE **AUTHOR**

ALEXIS BURLING

Alexis Burling has written dozens of articles and more than 35 books for young readers on a variety of topics, including current events, biographies of famous people, nutrition, and fitness. She is also a professional book critic with reviews of adult and young adult books, author interviews, and other publishing industry–related articles published in the *New York Times*, the *Washington Post Book World*, the *San Francisco Chronicle*, and more. Alexis lives in White Salmon, Washington, with her husband, cats, and hundreds of books.